BAD BLOOD

The First in the
Cycle of the Aphotic World

THE APHOTIC SERIES

Bad Blood
Out For Blood
Blood Loss
Blood Pact
Blood Relations
Flesh and Blood

BAD BLOOD

Tobin Elliott

To my daughter Madison, who thought this book was about her.
Thankfully, she was wrong.

To my son, Hunter, who could possibly have been the demon
child who did bad things.
Thankfully, he didn't.

And, of course, to my wife Karen,
who always reads this stuff, then gives me a weird, yet still
somehow loving look.

ACKNOWLEDGEMENTS

Thank you to everyone in my life who keeps me sane. You are my family. My blood…

To Ryan and Lisa Hickey, and your incredible family. You've given me over two decades of unwavering friendship. I've never laughed so much, or for so long, with anyone else. When I'm down, you bring me up. When I'm up, you lift me higher. Because of your generosity, support, and friendship, my world is brighter and my life is better.

To my daughter Madison and my son Hunter, brilliant and beautiful kids both. You infuriate me, make me belly laugh, drive me batshit, fill me with pride. And both of you in your own unique ways have taught me the importance of leading by example. You've inspired me to be a better father. I love you more than you'll ever know.

Finally, and most importantly, to Karen Elliott. My wife, my friend, my sparring partner, my sounding board, my shoulder to cry on, my friend to laugh with, my greatest critic and my biggest supporter. You stuck by me when you didn't need to; you picked me up when I was down. You challenged me to be the person I never thought I could be. I am what I am today because of you. For all of this and so much more, I love you, and I am *"…completely and perfectly and incandescently happy."*

PART ONE
GETTING ODD

"Come child, you have heard the voices,
and all is well…"

THE CRAWLING CHAOS
H. P. LOVECRAFT

CHAPTER ONE
SUMMER 1975

TALIA COULDN'T HELP it. Alex made her frustrated.

Not that Talia was all that crazy about *The Flintstones*, but jeepers, it was the only good show on besides stupid news or stupid game shows or other stupid stuff. And when she would try to watch it, Alex, her stupid baby sister, would crawl over to the TV, pull herself up the front, and slap the screen. Every time Fred Flintstone showed up, she'd squeal, "Fed! Fed! Fed!" and slap the screen some more.

She was stupid.

Talia kept yelling at her. "Lex! Lex! Get outta the way!"

She wouldn't dare call Alex stupid out loud, not with her mother in the other room making dinner. Mom would give her a good licking for that. Talia wasn't really sure why it was called that because when her mom would pull down her pants and spank her bum, it sure never felt like licking to her.

So, she chose to say it quietly to herself. "Stupid Lex."

And she was! The stupid kid couldn't walk, couldn't hardly talk, couldn't even poop on the toilet, but Mom always seemed to play with her more and talk to her more and hold her more.

Talia was a whole lot older than Alex. This September, she would be going into the fourth grade. So she was smart and she knew she was getting too old for Mom to hold and stuff. But she still kind of wanted her to.

Instead of moving out of the way, Alex stood directly in front of the TV screen, stock-still, no longer squealing, but grasping the top of the set and mumbling away to herself in stupid baby talk. Talia got madder at her stupid sister.

Alex couldn't do *anything*! She was so *boring*!

"Lex, you're making me frust-cher-ated!" she said, trying to sound very adult-like. "Get outta the *way*, Booger!"

"Talia!" Her mother's voice erupted from the other room. "No name-calling. You know she's younger than you. You have to be patient with her."

Yeah, she had to be patient with a stupid kid who didn't know anything except how to poop her pants and block Fred Flintstone.

Alex was the reason Dad left.

So Talia hated her.

Which is why, when Alex still didn't move, Talia decided to make her.

She slid as quietly as possible off the couch, but didn't move far. She worked to get the right amount of exasperation in her voice — not enough to make her mom come running, but not too little either.

"Lex!" she said. "Will you *please* move?" Yup, that "please" in there was *just* right.

As soon as she finished saying it, she got up behind Alex. The stupid baby was patting the screen again, little snaps of static electricity sounding from beneath her hands as she squealed, "Fed! Fed!"

Talia brought her hand up to the back of Alex's head, the feel of her baby-fine hair like the softest kitten, and snapped it forward, bouncing her sister's face off the screen.

Alex turned around, looked at Talia searchingly for a second before her lower lip curled down and her face scrunched up. Talia watched with fascination as her eyes grew big, fat tears.

2

She had to time it just right.

Alex opened her mouth wide and sucked in a big breath, her little tummy distending with the effort, and let out a ferocious wail. Her face darkened to pink, and then to angry red.

"Oh my gosh, Lex!" Talia said. "Are you okay?" Then she wrapped her arms around the stupid Booger in a big, sisterly hug. "It's okay," she said. "It's okay."

Mom came bounding around the corner, a dishcloth still in one hand. Her face was stern. "Talia! What did you do?"

She kept hugging the Booger. "I didn't do nothing!" she said, projecting as much innocence and care as she could. "She was watching Fred Flintstone and she tripped or something and bonked her head on the TV!"

Alex was bawling, wracking sobs that shook like tremors through her whole body.

Mom came over and Talia instinctively backed off.

Talia watched her mother's eyes grow wide. "Oh my god! Alex!" Talia looked over and saw the blood.

Oh jeez, she thought. *There's an awful lot of blood. Tons.*

As Alex cried, it alternately dribbled down her chin onto her favourite Mickey Mouse shirt along with gobs of spit, or it sprayed outward onto her mother's knees in a gross mist.

Shoot! Talia thought. *I didn't mean to do that!* She just wanted the Booger to shut up.

Then she thought, *Well, I guess that's what she gets when she doesn't listen.*

The three of them stood frozen, then Alex lifted her arms for Mom to pick her up, which, of course, Mom did. She didn't even care that she was getting blood all over herself. *That's all the Booger can do,* Talia thought. *But at least she can't tell on me.*

"Aw, sweetie, let's get some ice, okay?" Mom said.

Her mom took Alex into the kitchen, cooing soft words in that high voice that she only used with her. The one that sounded like she was smiling even though she wasn't.

Her mom hadn't smiled much since Dad left.

Stupid Booger. All her stupid fault.

Talia looked back at the TV. *The Flintstones* was over now, and some other stupid show was on. Talia slapped at the pull switch on the TV to shut it off. The picture first flattened, then squeezed down to a tiny bright spot.

There was a spot of blood just to the left of the fading point of light. Talia touched her finger to it. The warmth from the screen seemed to travel through the blood and up her arm. She felt a small prickling in her scalp and thought, *That blood is Alex's. And I made it happen.*

The prickling feeling grew, becoming more pleasurable. Talia closed her eyes and slowly, slowly, pulled her finger from the TV and put it in her mouth.

When she opened her eyes, seconds or minutes later, she saw something else.

Something that delighted her.

◆ ◆ ◆

THAT NIGHT, AFTER all the screeching and yelling had stopped, after her mom had held an ice cube wrapped in a facecloth to Alex's mouth, after dinner and baths and all that, Talia lay awake in bed, wrapped in warm bedclothes and cool, blue moonlight, her small night light offering just enough reassurance of safety.

Alex snored lightly in the crib across the room from her.

Talia reached down, squeezing her hand between the mattress and the box spring until she felt it. Then she pulled it out. She held the object up so that she could see it in the light.

She turned it over and over in her small fingers. So smooth. So shiny. Yet, it had a certain sharpness too. She scraped the edge of the thing along her fingers and felt it bump and catch against the ridges of her fingerprints.

It was hers now. A keepsake. A reminder that she was bigger than Alex. That she was smarter and stronger.

Talia fell asleep with Alex's baby tooth in her hand, her little fist wrapped tightly around it.

She never relaxed her grip on it at any time throughout the long night.

CHAPTER TWO
SUMMER 1975

TALIA SAT IN her room—well, really it was hers and Alex's, but it was more hers because she had been here first—trying to keep away from the Booger. They'd fought a lot recently and she didn't want to get into any more trouble with Mom.

But it was hard to not fight with her. Sometimes she just wished Alex would go away so it would be just her and Mom. Maybe Dad would come back then.

Talia missed her dad a whole lot.

Before Alex came along, it was just the three of them. And Mom would help her when she took her bath and she'd play Barbies with her and sometimes she would even dress her up, with makeup and everything.

Dad would have tea parties with her and take her on the scary rides at the carnival, the ones that Mom was too scared to ride. Talia and her dad would always climb into the seats, making fun of Mom, who would be standing outside of the ride with a fist up to her mouth, looking as if she was going to poop herself. They wouldn't ever tell her they made fun of her though. It was their little secret.

And Dad would also do her most favourite thing ever. Every night—well, every night until he started coming home real late—he would read her a story. Her favouritest of all had been *The Wizard of Oz*. She would giggle when he would make all the different voices, but it was his cackling, scary Wicked

Witch voice that she liked best. He would poke her tummy while he read as if he was trying to scare her, but mostly it just tickled and she always giggled.

And then, when they were done reading, and it was time to go to sleep, that's when her dad would shut off the light and they would wrestle, with Talia always trying to get an arm or leg out from under the covers while he frantically tried to keep her covered up. He would always huff and puff and pretend he was getting angry with her, but he never was. And when they finally settled down, he would tousle her hair and say, "Goodnight Poopypants." Then he would lean down and kiss her cheek. She loved the whiskery feel of his face against hers and the smell of him. She always took a big, deep breath whenever he hugged her. And then he would say, "Sweet dreams, baby. I love you," and he would just look at her, in the dark. He always looked kind of sad.

He did that every night.

But then Mom got pregnant and fat, and then she went to the hospital and they came home with stupid Alex.

After that, Dad didn't always have time to read to her because sometimes he had to do something with Alex.

And most of the time he didn't wrestle with her anymore — even when she begged him to. Instead, he just gave her a quick peck on the cheek and said, "G'night."

He didn't call her baby anymore, either.

And somehow, of all the things she missed, that was the worst.

Once Alex came home, it messed up everything. Talia always had to be quiet after school because Alex was napping. And she always had to watch TV with the sound so low that she couldn't hardly hear it.

Once Alex came home, Dad started *not* coming home. When he did, him and Mom would fight all the time. Or else they wouldn't talk at all, and then it seemed like the whole house was smaller and darker. She didn't like it when they didn't talk. Talia would always be extra quiet then, and extra good. She always thought she had done something bad and they'd gotten mad about it.

All she ever wanted to do when they acted like that was grab her mom's hand and her dad's hand and tell them to kiss and make the funny faces and the funny talk like they used to.

She'd thought about this a few times before Talia realized that it all seemed to start when Alex came along. So then she didn't like Alex that much. Oh yeah, she was cute and all, and sometimes when she laughed with her big, gummy, goobery mouth, Talia couldn't help but laugh too.

But mostly, she didn't like Alex that much. And sometimes, Talia hated her.

When Dad left, and her mom had said that he had to go away for a while, Talia knew he was going forever because he took a lot of stuff with him. He even took his favourite stuff, like his golf clubs, and Talia knew when you took your favourite stuff it was because you were scared to leave it behind in case you never got to see it or play with it again, so that meant you weren't coming back.

And she could tell when, after he had everything packed in the truck, he came back and tousled her hair and said, "Goodbye, Poopypants." He didn't just give her a kiss on the cheek then. He did that, but he hugged her and hugged her and hugged her. She felt his sandpapery whiskers on her face and smelled the good smell of him.

She breathed that good smell in, something in the back of her head telling her to pull it inside her, to hold it as long as she could and never forget that smell. And all the time she was trying to hold that smell of him, to lock down the memory of that smell, something fluttered in her chest. It felt awful.

Finally, he said, "I love you, baby. Be good for your mommy, okay?" Then he whispered something else, really low in her ear, that she couldn't quite make out.

It wasn't until he was in the truck and backing out of the driveway that she realized her cheek was all wet where he'd hugged her. She brought her hand to her cheek, swiped at the wetness, and looked at it.

Then she looked up and watched her dad drive away.

That's when she started to cry, because she knew for sure that he wasn't coming back, no matter what Mom said.

Because she figured out what he'd whispered to her.

He'd said, "I'm sorry. I can't fix it."

She didn't know what he couldn't fix, but she did know one thing.

She knew that it was Alex's fault.

So now Talia avoided her, staying in her room if Alex was out in the living room, or going out into the living room if Alex was in their room.

But she was bored. Bored, bored, *bored*!

Sitting on her bed, she looked around the room, wanting something to capture her attention, but nothing did. Her stuffed animals, which her mom called "stuffies," were all lined up on her bed, but she didn't want to play with them. There were boxes of games in her closet, but she needed more than one person to play and Marcia wasn't here yet and Mom was getting ready for work, so she couldn't. She didn't want to draw. She didn't feel like going outside.

She thought about holding the tooth again, but she didn't want her mom to catch her with it. That was her secret. No one could find out about it.

But just the thought of that tooth — that small, hard, shiny trophy — made a pleasant prickle across her scalp again. It was a pleasurable buzzing that relaxed her. She closed her eyes and enjoyed it.

Then she heard the doorbell chime.

That meant Marcia was here. *Something to do!*

She went out to greet Marcia and say goodbye to her mom.

◆ ◆ ◆

"Hey, Miz D!" Marcia Mayer said as she came through the front door. Alex scampered unsteadily toward her and Marcia scooped her up. "And aren't you a big bundle of smiles today!" Marcia laughed at her gap-toothed grin and boinked her lightly on the nose and Alex giggled, then squirmed to get away, so she put her back down.

"Hold on, kiddo," Marcia said. "Got something for ya." She reached into her bag and pulled out a plush Dino the Dinosaur from *The Flintstones*. Alex squealed with delight, grabbed it, mumbled "thangoo" and jammed Dino's head into her mouth, then scuttled off like an ungainly spider.

"Oh Marcia," Diane said, "you shouldn't have. You're gonna spoil them."

"Couldn't resist," Marcia said, smiling.

Talia ran to Marcia as well, wrapping her in a big hug. "Oh my goodness, Tal! Did you grow another few inches since I last saw you? Holy cow!" Talia beamed. "Got you something too!"

Talia bounced from foot to foot as Marcia reached into her bag again, then presented her with a book. "It's *Oh, The Thinks You Can Think!* by Dr. Seuss."

Talia's eyes grew wide. "I *love* Dr. Seuss!"

"I know. That's why I stopped by The Last Word bookshop and Mr. Holt helped me pick it out. When I saw it, I just knew it was the perfect book for you. It's brand new."

Marcia loved babysitting the girls, and knew how to make them happy.

Talia grabbed her hand. "Come read it with me!"

She did her best to pull Marcia to her room, tugging on her hand as though working to separate it from her wrist. "Hold on!" she laughed. "Hold on! Let me talk to your mom for a bit, then I promise I'll come read with you, okay?" Talia reluctantly agreed, scooting off with a smile on her face and the book in her hand.

♦ ♦ ♦

TALIA TOOK HER new book into her room. The first thing to do was to find a place on her shelf for it. Once it had a home, then she could read it. Her and Marcia.

She was going to put it with her other Seuss books—Talia had a lot of them. Five! But when she picked up the book to put it in its new home, it didn't feel right.

She put it on the mostly empty bottom shelf, the only book there. Its own special place.

Talia turned then, thinking maybe she could play with her secret hidden tooth for a minute, but before she could slip her hand between the mattress and box spring, she stopped.

There was something else in the room.

At first, Talia thought her mom had come in, but when she checked, she was still alone. Her eyes slid back to her bed again, almost against her will.

There was something in the room with her.

She couldn't see it, but she knew it was there.

She wasn't afraid.

Not even when it spoke to her.

~...looook aaaat mmmmeeee...~

Her eyes searched her room and, just as though someone was guiding her gaze, they slid across the bookshelf nestled between her bed and Alex's, all their books stacked neatly on the shelves. Dr. Seuss, The Berenstain Bears, Sesame

Street...and one she didn't recognize, sitting alone on the bottom shelf. A big book. Not *Oh, The Thinks You Can Think!*

At first, she couldn't read the title on its spine. Then, after blinking and rubbing her eyes—because looking at the book made her eyes feel funny—she realized there actually wasn't a title there at all. She walked over and pulled the book off the shelf and immediately dropped it.

The stupid thing was heavy! But it wasn't the weight of it that made it drop from her hand.

It was *warm*.

It felt icky...but at the same time, she kind of liked it. It made her feel like she had a secret that no one else knew. *Kinda like the tooth*, she thought. A small smile spread across her face.

Then she wondered, *Is the voice coming from the book?* She couldn't tell.

She bent over and picked up the book, ready for the heft of it this time, but it didn't seem anywhere near as heavy as she'd first thought. She sat down on the floor, her back to her bed, and placed it on her lap. The book covered her knees.

She sat for a moment, just looking at the cover. It still made her eyes feel weird, as though they were going in and out of focus, but it seemed to be lessening. At first, it looked like there was nothing she could read on the cover, just a bunch of strange letters that she couldn't make sense of. She was pretty sure they were called symbols—things that stood for other things, but she didn't know what those other things were. And she thought she saw shiny corners on it, too.

But then it all changed. And though Tal thought that should bother her in some way, it didn't. She wanted to think about it, but it seemed to keep squirming out of her thoughts, like minnows scooting through her fingers at the creek.

♦ ♦ ♦

"SORRY ABOUT THAT," Diane said. "They sure love you."

"That's okay, Miz D," Marcia said. "They're sweeties."

Diane looked at her skeptically. "For *you*, maybe." They shared a laugh.

"You working your four-to-midnight shift again?"

That got a weary sigh from Diane. "Yeah," she said, and Marcia could see how tired she was.

"Y'know, any time you want, I could come over early, or even stay all night, so you could get some more sleep."

"Oh girl, I can't afford a live-in babysitter."

Marcia gave her a look. "You don't have to pay me. I'm offering." She looked at Alex playing with her toys on the floor. "Besides, what else do I have to do this summer?"

"Oh, I'm sure a girl your age could get into all sorts of trouble," Diane said, smiling.

"Yeah, like a thirteen-year-old can do so much!" Marcia said, her voice thick with sarcasm. "*Especially* with my dad."

"Thirteen, already? Oh wait, your birthday was back in May, wasn't it?"

Marcia nodded, pleased that she remembered.

"And your dad is just looking out for you. Don't worry, in a few years you're going to want that kind of care again...and it doesn't always come in a boyfriend package." A sad look passed over Diane's face for just a second and then it was gone, like smoke. "Trust me on that one, kid."

Diane gathered her keys, jacket, and lunch. "I'm heading out, guys!" she said. Alex immediately scooted over, obviously knowing this would be the time for kisses and hugs. Talia trotted out, looking distracted, but broke into a run that ended with Diane scooping her up in a hug.

"Be good for Marcia," Diane said.

"I will," Talia said, drawing that last word out as she rolled her eyes dramatically.

13

"They're always good," Marcia said. She tickled Alex as she crawled by. "Aren't you, munchkin?" Alex let out a squeal and a giggle and trundled back to her toys.

Diane left some last-minute instructions on what to do with the dinner in the fridge and headed out. Marcia closed and locked the door behind her.

She turned to tell Talia that she could read with her now, but the girl had already disappeared back into the bedroom.

When she failed to emerge after a half-hour Marcia went to check on her, but when she saw her sitting with a book — probably the Seuss one — at the foot of her bed she decided to let her be. Marcia came back out to the living room and dug around in her purse until she found an envelope, a pad of paper, and a pen. She probably wouldn't get much of a letter written to Michelle, a friend of hers who was working overseas in a Bible camp, but she could get it started now before dinner and finish it off once the kids were in bed.

She didn't like to be asleep when Diane came home, as she wanted to always appear vigilant with her kids. Diane had given her heck for not crashing on the couch more than once, but Marcia just didn't feel right getting paid for babysitting while she was sleeping. So, writing a nice long letter to Michelle would help keep her up.

Alex demanded her attention a few times, and she gladly gave it. The kids were such sweeties and rarely misbehaved around her. She recalled some of the stories Diane told her, but had never really seen any of the bickering herself. She did notice that Alex had a bit of a fat lip, but she was also just learning to walk so that could have come from anywhere.

♦ ♦ ♦

WHEN TALIA HAD re-entered the bedroom, the book seemed to be waiting for her to pick it up again. She settled against the bed and pulled the book—she still couldn't decide if it was heavy or not—onto her lap.

Now she could read the cover. No pictures. Just seven words.

What thinks do you want to think?

Well that had a lot of answers, didn't it?

~…yeeeessss iiiit doessss…~

Again she wondered if it was the book talking to her.

Tal felt something bubbling up within her. Fear? Well, sort of, but then she heard that voice again.

~…nnnnoooo…~

And though she didn't know how it happened, that panicky feeling just dissolved and she felt fine again. Better than that, actually. She felt happy, like she'd made a brand new friend.

The feeling was exactly like when she'd first found the tooth and spent those first few minutes in her bed examining it. Exactly the same prickling in her scalp. But times a million. A *jillion*.

Talia opened the cover slowly and reverently, taking an almost perverse joy in delaying the unveiling of the book's contents.

◆ ◆ ◆

IT WAS JUST about supper time and Marcia hadn't seen or heard Talia in a while, so she set down her pen and paper and got up to check on her again. Before leaving the room, she glanced quickly at Alex and saw that she was deeply engrossed in undressing a couple of dolls. Marcia knew Alex'd be coming to her soon to re-dress them, just so she could do it all over again, but for now she seemed content.

Marcia walked down the short hall to the girls' room and peeked in. Tal hadn't moved. She was still sitting on the floor with a large book in her hands. Her lips were moving, but Marcia could hear no sound. Tal seemed completely oblivious to Marcia's presence.

Marcia leaned against the doorframe and watched the younger girl, a little disappointed she wasn't reading the book she'd given her. Talia slowly flipped the pages, one hand gently pulling up a page, the other smoothing the page down, then moving out of the way. *That thing's darn near as big as she is*, Marcia thought.

But, more than that, the book gave her the willies.

It seemed that every time Tal turned a page, Marcia got a glimpse of something...horrible. Something that made her flesh crawl, but then an instant later it was gone and in its place were some innocuous text and pictures.

And it didn't just happen once. It happened with every page flip.

Every single one.

Anyway, it's time for supper, so she can put the confounded thing down, Marcia thought.

"Tal?" she said.

Talia didn't respond. She just kept reading, her lips forming shapes while her right foot rocked back and forth, back and forth.

"Tal?" she repeated.

Nothing.

"Talia!" she said louder.

Tal looked up from the book and broke into a wide, beautiful smile. "Hey Marce," she said.

"Really into that book, huh?"

Tal looked down at the book in her lap like it was the first time she was seeing it. Then she hefted the front cover over and the book closed with a liquid thud. Marcia caught a glimpse of

16

something the colour of coffee and cream, and the cover had metal reinforced corners — she was sure of it — but in a blink it changed. It was now decorated with bright colours, animals circled around the title. *Oh, The Thinks You Can Think!* Marcia felt like she was blinking too much as she looked at it, like there was dust in her eyes.

What the heck?

Tal slid the book from her lap to the floor and its big cover slowly settled lower as the air escaped from between the pages. *There must be a few hundred pages there!* Marcia thought.

As Talia rose, Marcia got a better look at the book. It was the same slim tome, maybe twenty-five pages at best, that she'd bought from Mr. Holt two days ago at The Last Word. And not that big. Why had she thought it was big, like coffee-table book big? It obviously wasn't, but for just a minute there, Marcia would have sworn it was about the same size as the big, honking dictionary in the school library.

It didn't look like that now.

But it had a few seconds before.

Weird.

"Is it dinnertime?" Tal asked.

"Yep," she said. "That the book I got you?"

Tal looked at the book again. Every time she looked at it, it appeared as if she was seeing it for the very first time. There always seemed to be an element of surprise on her face when her eyes made contact with it.

She looked up at Marcia and shrugged. "Yup," she said. "What's for dinner?"

Marcia didn't sense that the girl was avoiding the subject. It seemed more that it was no big deal.

So she left it at that. *What the heck,* she thought. *It's just a book. At least she's reading.*

♦ ♦ ♦

TALIA PLAYED IT cool in front of Marcia. She didn't like lying to her. In fact, she really wanted to tell her all about it, but the Book told her not to. The Book told her lots of things.

~...aaaallll theeee thiiiinnnngssss weeee caaaan doooo toooogetherrrr...~

CHAPTER THREE
FALL 1975

DIANE'S EYES SNAPPED open, and a wave of panic washed over her. She shot an anxious glance at the clock above the television. Suppertime.

The house was far too quiet.

"Talia?" she called out. A quick run through the house told her what the fluttering in her chest had said all along: Talia wasn't home from school yet.

Frantic calls to the few children she considered Talia's friends confirmed that her daughter hadn't got sidetracked on the way home either. Diane threw some items into a diaper bag, scooped Alex out of the crib where she had been sleeping, and dropped her off next door with growly Mrs. Kovacs.

It took five stabs at the ignition before Diane slid the key home.

She stopped, dropped her head to the steering wheel, and took a bunch of deep breaths. If she didn't calm herself, she'd never find her daughter. She'd wrap the car around a tree, or worse. After taking a couple more breaths, she twisted the key. The motor chugged but didn't turn over.

With no warning it all came down on her again, even though it had been over a year now.

She was alone. Alone and raising two girls. Working a job she endlessly thought she was failing at.

Talia wasn't home yet, and she had no idea where her

daughter was. Obviously she couldn't do this parenting thing on her own.

She tried the key again. This time the big motor fired and she dropped the car into gear.

Damn her! Talia knows better than this. She always comes straight home from school. Always.

Oh god, she's got to be all right. Please let her be all right.

Damn, damn, DAMN!

Mrs. Kovacs hadn't said anything to her when she dropped Alex off—Diane preferred to use Marcia, but she lived too far away to be convenient in emergencies like this—but Mrs. Kovacs's silence had been clear: *Talia's been missing over two-and-a-half hours and you're just noticing now?*

Mrs. Kovacs just didn't understand how tired she was. Alex was barely a year old, and Talia...even at eight, Talia was a wrecking crew.

So when Alex went down for her nap, she was just going to rest on the couch for a bit and watch *All My Children*—she always saw some similarities between herself and the soap's Mona Kane, a single mother just like her, bringing up that spoiled brat, Erica. She remembered hoping that Talia and Alex wouldn't grow up like those Pine Valley kids, and then she must have dozed off. Now it was ten after six, no supper made, Talia missing, and Alex still sleeping in a dirty diaper. Which meant Mrs. Kovacs would have to change her immediately.

She was probably calling the police on Diane right now.

♦ ♦ ♦

PANIC ROSE IN her throat like an animal struggling to get itself loose. It had been half an hour and nothing. Going back and forth, back and forth over the route Tal would have taken to get from school to home. But there was more than one route.

20

She felt herself getting overwhelmed, losing control, but forced the panic down. She pictured herself holding it underwater and drowning it.

She'd even pulled over and asked two boys who were Marcia's age—Robert Bostash, her paperboy, and that poor, homely Dennis Bussik, all glasses and bowl cut, who had some funny nickname, the Frog or Lizard or something—but they assured her they had not seen Talia. They both seemed to pick up on her concern and looked nervous as they answered her questions. The Bostash boy suggested she may still be in the schoolyard.

God! I haven't even thought to get out of the car and check the schoolyard, she'd thought. *What kind of mother am I?*

Diane had hoped the boy was right. No, she *prayed* he was. He wasn't.

So the next place would be the park. She was probably there. She *had* to be there. *Oh Jesus, what if she wasn't there? What if somebody had come and...*

What if she was dead?

Her mind flashed back briefly to her ex-husband Glen's older brother Charlie in his casket, not too long after Glen had left Diane and the girls. Charlie and his younger brother Jude had tried to get Diane and Glen to reconcile. Diane had dutifully packed the girls and driven the two hours to Charlie's place.

Glen hadn't even shown up, and an hour after Diane and the kids had arrived paramedics were wheeling Charlie out on a stretcher.

The funeral was three days later. That was the last time she'd seen any of the Davis side of the family, including Glen. One brother grieving, the oldest brother dead, and the middle one that may as well have been.

Dead too soon. That's what everyone had said about Charlie. That's what everyone would say about Tal.

No, dammit. She's fine. Her baby was fine. She would find her on the swings, and she would smack her butt so hard…

But first she would kiss her and hug her and tell her how much she loved her.

She reached the park, the car slewing in a twisted skid on the gravel of the parking area. She killed the engine and stepped outside.

"Talia?" she called. "Tal?" Diane didn't like the shrillness in her voice, but couldn't seem to keep it away. "C'mon baby, Mommy's not mad. Mommy just wants you home. Talia? Honey?"

The evening air felt cold on her face. Not biting yet, but close. Snow would be here soon, she could smell it. The wind blew her long hair into her face. Leaves skittered playfully about her feet, as if dancing to a tune.

She pulled her sweater tighter around her. *Christ,* she asked herself again, *what kind of mother am I?* She couldn't even remember if Talia took her jacket this morning. *If Sgt. Flewwelling needs a description of what clothes she was wearing, I couldn't even give it to him!* She shivered violently.

"Tal?"

She'd entered the park just as the sky was darkening. *Maybe it's better that Glen's gone,* she thought. *If he were to come in the front door, looking for his kids and his dinner, what the hell would I tell him? "There's no dinner. Oh, and by the way, I lost one of the kids. No big deal, we have another one."*

Oh, Jesus. She was losing it. Her kid, and her mind.

The swings and the monkey bars were on the far side of the park, by the big old pine trees. She didn't see anyone over there, but it was a ways off. Talia could be lying on the grass watching the leaves, or maybe lying on her back with her dress up around her waist, and her underwear…

She heard a high-pitched scream that abruptly cut off. She started to run.

"Talia? Talia! OmigodTalwhere*ARE*you?"

"Mom? I'm in here, Mom."

She screamed Talia's name so loud that she almost drowned out her daughter's voice. Her baby was all right!

Frantically, she pushed her way through the sagging pines. The first thing that hit her was the smell.

"Mr. Squirrel's dead, Mom."

An animal's entrails were strewn all over the pine-needle carpet. Everywhere. Steaming in the cool evening air.

But none of the carnage was on Talia. Not one speck of blood. Her baby was fine. She sobbed as Talia stood and stepped into her open arms. The pretty pink dress that Glen's mom had given Talia for Christmas last year had pine gum on it, and she smelled of the mess on the ground, but otherwise she seemed completely unscathed. She hugged Talia tight. Almost too tight. Talia started to squirm, so she reluctantly let her go.

"He was my friend, Mom. But now he's dead."

"Yes he is honey, and if you ever pull a stunt like this again, I'll kill you." It was something that she regretted saying instantly. That was the panic talking, not her.

She softened her voice. "C'mon, baby, let's get home."

♦ ♦ ♦

AS HER MOM marched her to the car, Talia knew she was mad, and usually that would both worry and upset her, but right now it did neither. She was too busy thinking about what had happened under the pine tree before her mother had found her.

Talia looked behind her, Mr. Squirrel was back there. Now he was bird food. He had been bad, so she had punished him.

23

She hadn't meant to. Not at first. She'd just wanted some time by herself.

She had been walking home from school and thought of Alex waiting for her at home. She had decided that she didn't want to see Alex just quite yet.

When Talia found the big pine tree with the branches that reached the ground, she just knew it would be a perfect spot to get some time away from her sister. She crawled under the branches, then sat down on a bed of coppery-gold pine needles. The branches drooped so low nobody could see in, but she could see out. She took a deep breath. She loved the smell. It was perfect in here.

Quiet.

No Alex. She sighed in contentment.

Maybe if she got home a little later, she wouldn't have to look at her sister's cutesy little face waiting for her in the front yard, where she was probably playing with Mr. Whiskers. Talia used to like Mr. Whiskers, but now that cat seemed to have a big hate-on for her.

So she hated that cat now.

Just like Alex. Just like her Unca Charlie. She knew it was supposed to be "uncle," but she couldn't say that when she was younger and now everyone called him that. He always kissed her too much. Unca Charlie made her feel funny — not like the Book funny, but a different and bad kind of funny — and wrong inside, and she didn't like it and she didn't like him neither.

She wasn't sad he was dead. He'd smelled bad. Like cigarettes —

A flicker of movement broke her thoughts.

Oh boy! A new playmate? she thought. *Maybe I can try out some more stuff from the Book!*

Talia watched the big black squirrel. It did that weird stop-start-stop thing that they do. *Why do they do that?* she wondered. It was like someone kept switching them off and on, off and on. *Click, click.*

It must have been gathering nuts for the winter. Its cheeks were bulging out, big and round. She smiled. *Just like Unca Charlie's*, she thought.

She wondered if she could get Mr. Squirrel to come over and play with her. She sure would like to pet that big, twitchy, fluffy tail. It looked so soft.

She squinted her eyes to tight slits, and clenched her fists into hard little balls. Hard enough to draw blood. Just like the Book had taught her.

Blood was important.

Mis-ter Squir-rel, she called. But only in her head.

Mr. Squirrel continued to do his stop-start-stop hop. Talia reached out and *pulled*. In mid-hop, the squirrel froze and then, slowly, it lost its balance. The animal toppled onto its side, the little body heaving.

The Book had taught her lots of stuff since she'd got It. She'd had It a long time now, since summer started, and that was like *years* ago!

It was the best book she'd ever had. It told her stuff that had helped her with Unca Charlie.

And now she had a new playmate to try some more of that stuff on.

Talia focused on Mr. Squirrel again, making him stand up and drop all of the stuff in his mouth. *Wouldn't want him to choke.* The nuts sprayed across the pine needles like thrown dice. Then she made him come over to the tree where she was sitting. Mr. Squirrel wasn't doing that stop-start-stop thing anymore. He just walked over, but kind of shaky-like. Sort of like Alex's toy doggy at home. Talia hated that thing too. It shook and wiggled and barked and made all sorts of noise, but it sure didn't act like a dog. Mom said they couldn't get a real dog. They couldn't afford it, she said.

That was probably because of all the money they spent on Alex's diapers and stuff. The Booger was such a pain in the butt.

The squirrel's mind was white with fear. His heart was pounding. Tal knew it. She was right there with the squirrel, not inside its brain, but sort of right beside it. She knew that when the heart went *bobbity bobbity bobbity* it was going much too fast. Tal remembered a couple of months ago, they had visited the Kelsos', who had a gerbil named Dammit — but they kept saying it was called Danny whenever the kids were around — and Tal had seen it drop dead when its heart did that. She had felt it then, too. She had only been trying to get it to do some tricks. Some stuff from the Book. But it got scared and its heart thumped way too fast and it just wouldn't slow down.

Then it stopped. Talia felt it kind of explode. She figured it might have been her fault. By accident.

She couldn't get Dammit to do *anything* after that had happened. Well, she made him twitch a bit, but that was it. And that was boring.

So, she reached out with her mind and slowed Mr. Squirrel's heart down, but not too much. She knew what happened when she did that too. That's how Unca Charlie died. But that hadn't been an accident. Not exactly.

Mr. Squirrel's eyes rolled up into his head. He kept jerking like a dog on a leash, like he was trying to get away. Talia had trouble controlling him. He wasn't being very much fun. But he was so cute!

She forced him to climb up onto her lap, and then she reached down to stroke his pretty tail. She'd never pet a squirrel before. It was going to be so soft, she could just tell. He was *sooo* pretty.

Her concentration lapsed, just for a second.

The squirrel spun and snapped at her hand.

26

Talia reacted without thought. Just as the squirrel's mind had been white with fear, Talia's mind went black with rage.

It was over in seconds. The squirrel, sensing its advantage, jumped from her lap, but her blackness cleared and she reached out with her mind again and stopped it mid-stride.

Then she forced its tail—that big, fluffy tail—around and into the squirrel.

Then she pulled it through the length of its body.

Quickly. Savagely. Just like the Book taught her.

In the end, while she had enjoyed getting back at Mr. Squirrel for biting her, there was one thing that had been truly fun. When she had made his pretty tail come out of his mouth, the squirrel had let out a short, high, loud scream. She didn't know anything could make a sound like that.

But then, she had never turned anything inside out before.

The next sound she was aware of was her mother's voice.

"Talia? Talia! OmigodTalwhere*ARE*you?"

Oh geez, Talia thought. *I forgot about going home.*

She knew she was in big trouble. Her first thought was to not say anything, but Mom sounded pretty freaked out, so she figured she'd better answer.

"Mom? I'm in here, Mom."

◆ ◆ ◆

CLIMBING INTO THE car, she took one last look at the big pine tree while her mother came around to the driver's side.

Talia allowed herself a small smile.

But she tucked it away again before her mother could see it when she got into the car.

27

CHAPTER FOUR
SPRING 1976

TALIA NEVER CARED much for Mrs. Kovacs. She was a mean old lady, with thick dark-framed glasses like a man would wear. And she had a moustache. And she yelled a lot. But the worst was, every spring and summer, it seemed that whenever Talia went outside, Mrs. Kovacs would be out there with her ugly, fat little dog. It would waddle behind her as she plucked weeds or whatever. Mrs. Kovacs was *always* bending down, and Talia would see nothing but her big, fat butt sticking up in the air.

Both her and her stupid dog Benji had big, fat butts. It was gross.

Talia's mom said she bent over a lot because she talked out of her ass. But she always told Talia not to repeat that. Talia thought Mrs. Kovacs yelled out of her ass.

And ever since that time when Tal was late coming home from school and Mom had gone out looking for her, Mrs. Kovacs seemed even meaner and nastier, if that was even possible.

Talia did like Mr. Kovacs. She didn't see him that much, but whenever she did — and Mrs. Kovacs wasn't bent over and yelling at him — he always smiled and waved to her. Whenever he said something, which really wasn't all that often, it was always something nice, like how great her hair looked, or how pretty her dress was.

She really liked Mr. Kovacs. She felt sorry for him,

having to put up with a fat old wife like that. Her and her fat old dog.

The one she used to like the most was Mr. Whiskers, the Kovacses' cat. He was lean and long and black and white, with one blue eye and one green one. Mrs. Kovacs had Benji, but Mr. Whiskers was Mr. Kovacs's favourite pet.

Whenever Talia came home from school, Mr. Whiskers always sat waiting for her at the end of their front porch, and as soon as she reached the sidewalk in front of their house, he would step quickly but daintily down onto the grass with a jaunty bounce that always made her giggle. Then he'd come up to her and wind his way around her legs. Mr. Kovacs always said he was "just trying to get a little lovin'," which Talia thought was funny.

That was all before last summer. For some reason, now, whenever Talia walked by the Kovacses' house, Mr. Whiskers would prowl up close, but never close enough to reach, and yowl at her. If she moved too suddenly, he would arch his back, fluff up his tail, and hiss, ears flattened back on his head. He'd do that weird sideways walk, crabbing away from her.

It was like he suddenly hated her.

If Mr. Kovacs witnessed this, he would always yell at the cat and wave his arms. When he did this, Mr. Whiskers would bound across the yard and slip under the fence.

It bugged her at first, but eventually, as it wore on, Talia came to accept it. She didn't like it, didn't ever really get used to it, but she accepted it.

Until today.

When she arrived home from school, she could see Marcia had already picked up the Booger from daycare. The day was lovely and warm, and the two of them were sitting in the front yard. Marce was in a lawn chair reading a magazine and the Booger was playing with Mr. Whiskers.

She had a string that she dragged through the grass and Mr. Whiskers stalked it like a panther, scooching his face down in between the blades of grass, his eyes wide and dark, while his butt stuck up in the air and wiggled before pouncing. The Booger laughed and laughed at the cat, and the cat never grew bored of this simple game.

Tal stood well back on the sidewalk, watching. She couldn't help but smile at how absurd the cat looked when he wiggled his butt, and how he made Alex shriek with laughter.

Then Marcia looked up from her magazine and spotted her. "Hey Tal!"

"Hey Marce," she answered.

At the sound of her voice, Mr. Whiskers stopped and spun, his butt still in the air, his tail fluffed. Talia could even see his raised hackles.

Marcia didn't seem to notice. She scooped up Alex, walked up the steps, and opened the screen door. "Come on inside and wash up, Tal," she said. "Your mom'll be home soon. I'll get you some pink lemonade." With that, she turned and entered the house.

And Mr. Whiskers attacked.

◆ ◆ ◆

WHEN IT WAS all over, Talia took the time to look around. She'd been lucky no one had been outside or watching, at least not that she could see.

She was pretty impressed with what she had done, though.

It was cool how, just as the cat leapt for her face, all fangs and claws, she'd reached out, *pushed*, and stopped the cat mid-jump. It hung there, initially furious, then increasingly frantic. She felt it in her head, just like she had with Mr. Squirrel.

It started to pant, its tongue sliding in and out of its still-open mouth. Talia approached the cat, still hanging at least three feet off the ground. The only things that moved were its tongue, its frantically searching miscoloured eyes, its heaving sides, and its tail, snapping jerkily every once in a while, causing it to turn slowly one way or the other.

Talia reached out and stroked Mr. Whiskers's head, then moved to scratch behind his ears and down along his jaw where it used to make him purr. She thought of petting his fluffy tail — just like Mr. Squirrel's, only fluffier. But, instead of purring, the creature hissed as a hot stream of piss jetted from its body.

She could feel its desire to bite, to scratch, and to kill her if it could. Also, over all of that desire, she felt its unrelenting need to escape.

She would let it do none of that.

"I used to love you, Mr. Whiskers," she said, stroking his smooth back. He would dip a little bit in the air when she did that, but she would just mentally reach out and push again to bring him back up.

"I used to," she said, "but I don't anymore."

She stopped petting him and stood, observing him instead. Taking him in for the last time. She decided she wanted something to remember him by. A souvenir. And she knew just what she wanted.

She reached unhesitatingly into the cat's still-open mouth, pinched one of his fangs between her thumb and forefinger, and pulled. The stupid cat came with it, so she gripped his scruff with her other hand and twisted the tooth.

It snapped just like when her and Mom pulled on a wishbone. Mr. Whiskers let out a low moan and his eyes rolled up in his head.

She let go of the cat and shook loose the sweaty fur that clung to her palm. Then she looked down at the broken tooth in her other hand before pocketing it.

31

So that was it. She was done with Mr. Whiskers. She walked away from him, toward her front door, but her mind was still on the paralyzed, suspended cat.

Then, she punished him. Not like the squirrel. She was growing up, getting smarter. She could *feel* herself getting smarter. The more she listened to her sister, the more Alex sounded like a baby.

So she tried something new. Something more...*mature*.

Just like the Book had taught her.

♦ ♦ ♦

DIANE OPENED THE door on her rustbucket '69 Impala, stepped out, and snagged her brand new, just-out-of-the-package-this-morning nylons on a rough chunk of scabrous metal jutting from beneath the door. She felt it scrape across her calf.

At least she didn't hack her leg open and have to bundle both girls up for a trip to the hospital to get a shot of something that would stop her leg from falling off.

It had been that kind of a damn day. Again. As usual.

She wanted to slam the door of the car, but figured it would just fall off, so she closed it normally. Okay, maybe a bit more forcefully than normal. Again, she silently thanked Glen for taking the fifteen-year-old Volkswagen Bug and leaving her with the Impala when he'd left. They had always planned on buying new, but could only ever afford something a few years old. Of the two pieces of shit, the seven-year-old Impala was still the more dependable. "For the girls," he had said. "To keep them safe." *Yeah, well,* she thought, *thanks for that. They needed a dad to keep them safe, too.*

But that hadn't stopped him from packing up his share of stuff from their broken-down, decade-long marriage and bolting. Then again, he claimed his running was keeping them safe. Diane took that as more of an excuse—his need to run outweighing his share of responsibility.

She sighed and tried to forget about it. This line of thinking was just going to lead her down a rathole and piss her off more than this day had already conspired to do.

Instead, she gathered her jacket and lunch bag from the back seat, put a smile on her face for Marcia and the kids, and turned to head up the walk.

When Diane wheeled around, jacket in one hand, lunch bag and keys in the other, she caught sight of a small black-and-red...something...that lay crumpled on the front steps of her house.

She figured it—whatever it was—probably belonged to Talia. That kid was always dropping things and losing them. When she'd been younger, Diane and Glen had figured she'd grow out of it, but, all these years later, she'd shown no signs of slowing down. It would probably be one of those unique and charming personality traits that some guy would fall in love with a long time from now.

With that, a real smile came to rest on Diane's face. *God, the kid's not even nine years old and I'm already marrying her off!*

Drawing closer to the bundle, she still couldn't make out what it was. Her mind struggled to match the awkward shape and colours with something familiar and understood.

Then Diane was at the bottom step. The thing sat two steps up, only one from the top. It looked sort of...silky, maybe? The evening sun hit it at an oblique angle. She dropped lightly to one knee—*what the hell, the pantyhose are ruined anyway*, she thought—and that's when her eye caught something recognizable.

A paw.

A cat's paw.

But this couldn't be a cat. The shape was all wrong. If it was a cat, it would be a Picasso painting come to life.

She bent closer. She took it in, horrible as it seemed, but the absolute unreality of the sight actually kept the fear and disgust at bay, simply because it could not be an animal she was looking at. She saw it, but she didn't comprehend it. *A stuffie of some sort?*

She stayed like that for a few seconds, unblinking, her brows knitted together in concentration.

Then the thing opened an eye and shivered. Then it moaned.

It took Diane a few minutes of breathing, of just sitting and focusing on getting air in and out of her lungs, before she could even consider what the hell lay on her doorstep. But finally she got herself under control. She thought about calling Marcia out, but she knew the kids would follow and they definitely didn't need to see this.

She cursed Glen yet again. *Damn him!* This would be a Glen thing if he was still around. But he wasn't. So it was down to her.

She gathered her feet under her and stood up. A little shaky, but okay. She approached the thing again.

God, what a mess.

If this was a cat, it looked like someone had tried to fold it just forward of the hips, to bring the right rear leg around to almost meet the right shoulder of the front legs. But then, that section also appeared folded.

Parts of the poor thing were split open and leaking. Not just blood, but more solid, fleshy things.

Viscera. The word roiled into her mind and conspired to make her stomach churn even worse.

How can it still be alive?

It must have been hit by a car, Diane thought, but she couldn't figure how it got halfway up her steps. Thrown to the curb, okay. Even to the grass, if the car was moving fast enough. She'd once had a cat herself that had crawled back home on its front legs after its hips had been broken. But it had been incapable of climbing stairs, and it had been in much better shape than this one was.

She would have to do something about it before the kids saw. And she'd have to put it out of its misery.

Hands shaking, she picked up the items she'd dropped and went back to the car, placing them on the hood. Keys in hand, she headed for the side entrance to her garage.

Inside, the late afternoon sun shone through the small side window, illuminating the various bits of her stored life in a soft, warm glow, like a fond memory. She chose her steps carefully, not wanting to alert the kids that she was home just yet. Near the main entrance to the garage, stuck in a metal garbage pail with the other gardening tools, was a rusty shovel. She pulled it free.

She made her way back outside and around to the front steps again. The cat's single green eye stared at her like an accusation.

How the hell am I –

"You're dressed awful nice to be gardening, Mrs. Davis."

Diane turned, shovel raised slightly in alarm.

"Mr. Kovacs." She breathed a sigh of relief. "I'm sorry, you startled me." Mr. Kovacs stood in his yard, a cigarette in one hand, a dripping sprinkler attached to a hopelessly snarled green garden hose in the other.

"Sorry 'bout that," he said, flicking ash onto his lawn. Diane knew he didn't give two shits about the yard, but Mrs. Kovacs demanded green carpeted perfection.

"It's okay, don't worry about it," she said. "It's just this…I'm sort of rattled because…" She paused, considering. "Mr. Kovacs, could you help me for a minute?"

He smiled as though he'd been waiting for her request for weeks. "Of course! Of course!" he said. He dropped the sprinkler, then took one last drag off his cigarette before carefully pinching it between two calloused fingers and flicking it into the street.

He headed over briskly, and Diane didn't miss his quick glance to his front window. No Mrs. Kovacs. They were safe.

He approached, eyes on the shovel. As usual, Diane smelled the not-unpleasant odours of nicotine, sweat, and garlic on the man. On anyone else, it would have been repulsive, or at least off-putting, but on him, it seemed somehow comforting and homey. Fatherly.

"What can I do for you?" he asked.

"I've got a problem," she said, moving slightly to draw his attention to the animal, "that I don't want the girls to see."

Kovacs squinted. "What is that?"

"I think it's a cat. And it's really hurt, but still alive."

"A cat?" With that, he went to the porch and bent down to get a closer look. Diane followed suit.

"Ah geez," he said. "Ah geez."

"I know," she said.

"Mr. Whiskers?" he said.

"What?" Diane said. "No!" She looked closer at the animal. *Oh shit!*

"Oh god, Mr. Kovacs!" Tears welled up in her eyes. "I didn't know! I...didn't even realize! I never would have—"

He stayed that way for a while, bent over, hands on knees. His lips moved, but Diane didn't hear anything come out of his mouth. She stood uncomfortably beside him, not knowing what to do or say. Her hand fluttered, almost touched his arm, pulled away before contact.

Finally, he lifted a hand, wiped his eyes, then his nose, and then held the hand out to her. She almost took it in her own, fluttering again before she realized that he wanted her to pass him the shovel, which hung forgotten in her other hand. She handed it over. The hand that took it wasn't gentle.

He hefted the shovel once, as if to gauge its weight, then he placed the blade at the edge of the step. The rusted metal rasped as he slid it forward underneath the broken creature.

Mr. Whiskers let out a low moan that froze both of them, and Mr. Kovacs said, "ah geez" again. Diane noticed the cat only had three of its fangs. One was missing, probably broken off when the car, or whatever, had hit it. She had time to think, *Why am I noticing that, of all things, at a time like this?* before Mr. Kovacs reached forward and, with great care, put a hand behind the cat and maneuvered him onto the shovel. As he let go, he let out a soft "gah" sound.

By now, Diane's tears were falling freely. "Mr. Kovacs, I'm so sorry. I...I honestly didn't know it was...your cat."

It was as though he hadn't heard her. "I'll need your shovel for a few minutes," he said. "I'll return it later this evening if that's okay?"

"Of course," she told him. "What can I do to help?"

Mr. Kovacs said nothing. He just turned and headed between their two houses toward his backyard.

She watched him leave, stooped with the weight of his horrid cargo, until he rounded the corner and disappeared from her sight. Then she stood, not moving, for a little longer.

Finally, she roused herself, pulled out her own garden hose, and sprayed down the step as best she could. She managed to wash away the chunks and bits of...viscera. That word again. By the time she had finished there was a slightly darker patch on the step, but nothing noticeable unless someone was looking for it.

Satisfied, she shut off the water, coiled the hose, and found herself waiting for Mr. Kovacs to reappear.

When he still hadn't done so after twenty minutes, she picked up her things from the car, put on a happy mask, and entered her house.

♦ ♦ ♦

SHE FOUND HER shovel leaning against her garage door the next morning. It had been cleaned.

No trace of the animal was left on it.

PART TWO
GETTING EVEN

"I felt myself on the edge of the world; peering over the rim
into a fathomless chaos of eternal night."

DAGON
H. P. LOVECRAFT

CHAPTER FIVE
SUMMER 1976

SUMMER IN NEW Hope was a glorious time. The sky seemed to be forever blue, there was always enough of a breeze to make the leaves whisper, and enough heat to bring the strange electric buzzing of the cicadas. There were lakes to swim in and ice cream cones to eat. There was corn on the cob and hamburgers and cold Cokes. Bikes to ride, *Archie* comics to read. Campfires and sleeping bags and sleepovers, and long, hot days and cool nights to do it all in.

But Talia had no interest in any of it anymore.

There was only the Book. And the Book was all.

She had no idea when she stopped thinking of It as a book and started thinking of It as the Book.

Maybe after Dammit the gerbil.

Maybe after Unca Charlie.

Maybe after Mr. Squirrel.

Or maybe after Mr. Whiskers.

She wasn't sure any more. Things had changed a lot.

It had come on so subtly. It felt as though her eyes and her mind had been opened wider and wider. Stretched. At first it had felt as though she had been trying to drink from a high-pressure hose, but over time that overwhelming quality felt less so. She didn't know if she was catching up to the Book, or if the Book had got to know her better and was slowing down to her speed.

Either way, it was a lot better now.

And it had some pretty interesting side effects.

She'd felt herself getting smarter for a while now, but recently she'd begun feeling more mature as well. Maturity to back up those newfound smarts. The Book was feeding her so much.

In fact, it was as if the world had jumped into a hyperfocused reality.

Before, her vision had been limited, as though she'd had blinders on. Now, she could see farther and clearer, and with so much more breadth.

But it wasn't seeing, exactly. *It's…what? Sensing? Understanding? Knowing? Whatever it is, it's good. Hell, it's fucking great!*

Though, the downside was Talia suspected her mom knew something was up. It was nothing she said exactly, but there were times when Talia would say something—nothing especially strange—just…well…*anything* now, and her mom would get this particular *look* on her face. Pursed lips, narrowed eyes, like she was studying Talia, trying to spot the differences. She knew she was pissing her mom off with some of her comments, but it was just how she talked now.

She talked like an adult. Someone worthy of the Book.

On the plus side, her mother had been ecstatically happy with her grades by the end of the year. Her marks had rocketed straight to the top, and her report card was filled with glowing praise for her improvement, though each comment seemed to be tempered with the suggestion that she participate more in class, as she obviously knew the answers.

Participate more in class. Talia had to laugh at that one. No one would talk to her anymore. She was a virtual pariah in her school. Everyone just seemed to shy away from her. She'd get that same look from her teachers as she got from her mother. She could see it in their minds—*Why does Talia sound so different?*

42

They were probably just jealous that she was so intelligent. That's what the Book told her. And the Book was always right.

She knew that jealousy was part of it. But there was a lot more to it than that. Talia knew this because she realized a few months ago that she could see into people — just like she could see into the squirrel and Mr. Whiskers.

She knew her nickname around school was "the Spook" or "Spooky Talia" now. It's mostly what she got whenever she looked into anyone around her. They thought she was creepy.

She didn't bother looking into Alex's mind. She tried it a couple of times, but she really didn't get much of anything other than a headache from the crazy miasma — she liked that word, the Book had taught her that one — of thoughts, questions, and images. It was far too chaotic to keep looking at, so she stayed away from Alex's head.

Her mom wasn't much better. Talia knew she worried about money, about Alex and her, and that she was lonely. Her mind was usually a deep-brown funk. But Tal had seen it brighten and clear away like a sunrise.

When Alex did something cute. That was the only time.

That pissed Talia off. Nothing for her, only Alex. Even with all she had accomplished lately.

The bitch.

Tal found out what had happened with Mr. Whiskers's folded-up body by looking into her mom. It looked like it'd got poor Mr. Kovacs pretty upset. She knew he wondered just what had happened to his cat. It was pretty obvious no car could have done that. She could see his mind clench just a little whenever her mom saw him and said hi. He was just as friendly as ever on the outside, but he'd darkened up within.

Wasn't *that* interesting?

Talia didn't like that he was different on the inside than he was on the outside. So she found she was liking Mr. Kovacs less and less. It was disappointing that he was just like everyone else.

Marcia seemed to be the only one that didn't really look at Talia differently.

She'd obviously noticed some changes, but she put it down to Talia growing up. Talia knew Marcia prayed for her and worried about her, but it was always in a good way.

The whole praying thing was bullshit as far as Talia was concerned, but at least it was genuine from Marce's point of view and she did it out of love.

So really, aside from Marcia, Talia didn't have much use for those around her.

And that was fine with her. All she really needed was the Book.

It was her best friend.

Fuck, It's my only friend.

Talia hadn't been sleeping all that well lately. She found she was waking up a few times a night, knowing she'd had a terrible nightmare, but unable to remember any details about it. There was just the post-nightmare evidence: the bedclothes in knots, her pajamas soaked with sweat, her hands shaking, her mouth dry and foul-tasting.

She would calm herself with a few long, slow breaths before walking to the kitchen to get a drink. Then she would straighten out her bed and climb back in again. Sometimes she would pull out the teeth, one small and rounded, the other a sharp, curved arc. She wished she'd gotten one from Unca Charlie. And Dammit the gerbil and Mr. Squirrel, too. Just holding them in her hands seemed to calm her. When she was done she always made sure to hide them again before falling back asleep.

If she was lucky, she'd be out until morning, but most nights she woke up again a short time later in the exact same fashion.

It was after one of these mostly sleepless nights that everything started to go wrong. Her mom had called her down for breakfast three or four times and each time she hollered for her, she got a little louder about it. That pissed Talia off.

Then Tal went to the bathroom and discovered she'd gotten her third damn period. She didn't think she was supposed to get that for a couple more years yet. So that was pissing her off too, though the Book seemed to like the blood.

Then she walked into the kitchen, straight into the brown funk in her mom's head and the chaotic swirl of Alex feeding herself Cheerios with two delicate fingers.

"Morning, sleepyhead," her mom said. "What would you like for breakfast?"

What she really needed was a goddamn coffee, but she knew her mother wouldn't give her that.

"Just some toast?" she said.

"Oh honey," her mother said. "You have to eat more than that."

No, I really don't, Talia thought. *Leave me the fuck alone, why don't you?*

"I'll scramble a couple of eggs for you. You like eggs." Like she had to be told and, quite frankly, today she didn't like eggs.

"Mommy!" Alex squeaked.

"No, Mom," Tal said. "I don't want any eggs. Really, just some toast."

"Mommy!" Goddamn Alex again.

"How about some cereal, then? We've got Cheerios and Wh—"

"I don't want cereal either. I don't even want the toast, okay?"

"Mommy!"

"Honey," her mother said, and Talia felt that brown funk grow darker. "What's the matter?"

"Mommy!"

45

"Nothing's the matter. I'm just not hungry!" She stopped herself short of tacking a "Jesus!" onto the end of that.

"Mommy!"

"Don't you raise your voice to me, little miss!" Darker and darker.

"Mommy! Loooooook!"

"What is it, Alex?" Talia watched as her mom looked over at Alex. She was holding two Cheerios up to her eyes like small, crunchy eyeglass frames.

That's when the darkness blew away from her mother's mind.

Talia watched as it receded like a passing storm front being blown out to sea, leaving only sunshine and fucking rainbows in its wake. She cringed as she felt the smile welling up in her mother's brain long before it ever hit her face.

Night to day.

Sad to glad.

Pick any fucking metaphor there is, Talia thought. *She never does that for me anymore. Only for Lex.*

Talia stood in the middle of the kitchen, forgotten by her mother as she laughed and went over to hug Alex. That was something that Talia felt too. She felt herself disappear from her own mother's thoughts as though she wasn't standing three feet from where they were locked in a hug so sugary-sweet that Talia felt a diabetic seizure coming on.

Mom never hugs me like that anymore. Not ever.

Only the Booger.

Alex was giggling as her mother let her go and stood up.

"Hugs, Mommy, hugs," she pleaded, putting her hands up again.

Yeah, I'll give you hugs, Talia thought.

There were two sharp, distinct cracks, like twin gunshots going off, and Alex's arms fell at strange angles, one hitting and toppling her bowl of Cheerios before coming to rest on the white plastic tray in front of her. The other hung limply beside her.

Alex let out little squeak. Then she looked at her mother and Talia watched her face redden and crumple, her eyes scrunch up, and her mouth open wide to reveal her teeth. One prominently missing.

"What's the matter, Lex?" her mother said. And then the screaming started.

Talia turned and left the room. It was the only way she could hide the smirk.

◆ ◆ ◆

ONE SECOND, LEX was fine, the next she wailed like the hounds of hell were on her heels. "Lex?" Diane turned to Talia to see if she knew what had set her off, but only saw her daughter's retreating back. "Talia!"

Talia kept walking. She'd have to deal with her later.

Diane unlocked the tray, pulled it loose, quickly undid the safety straps, and grabbed Alex under the armpits. As she lifted her, she knew something was wrong.

Alex wasn't reaching for her. Alex wasn't putting her arms up.

They hung limply at her sides.

Balancing the girl on her hip, Diane took one of Alex's wrists and lifted her arm. Alex's walling ratcheted up several more notches.

"What's the matter, baby?" Diane said, tears springing to her eyes. "What's the matter with your arm, honey?"

But she already knew. She knew it was broken.

Gently, she felt up Alex's arm from the wrist. At mid-forearm, she felt the break. She literally felt the bones grinding against each other.

How the hell...?

Screw it. There'd be time for that later.

"Talia?" she called. No answer. "Talia!"

"What?" The word sharply bitten off.

What is with this attitude lately? Doesn't she realize her sister is in pain? Can't she hear her sister freaking? Alex continued to screech in her ear. It made her head throb.

"Go next door to Mrs. Kovacs's place and see if she can watch you. Tell her there's something wrong with Alex and I have to take her to Emergency."

"No!" came the voice from the other room. "I hate Crabby Kovacs!"

"No you don't!" Diane collected her purse and Alex's travel bag, always packed and ready by the door. "Dammit, Talia! Go! Now!"

Talia came stomping back into the kitchen, her face a mask of black emotions. Her eyebrows were furrowed down to a shallow "V," and the look on her face would almost be comic if the situation wasn't so dire. She grabbed her flip-flops from the mat, threw them down with a sharp slap, and slid her toes between the straps.

"Take your key. I don't know how long I'm gonna be."

"Why can't Marcia come over?"

"Do you *hear* your sister?" Talia just looked at her. "I don't have time to wait for Marcia to get over here. Maybe I can call her from the hospital." She took a second to calm herself down. "Honey, please. Your sister's in a lot of pain right now and I need to get her to the hospital to get her fixed up, okay? Please?"

"I guess," Talia said, her face dark. "I still hate Mrs. Kovacs. And her stupid dog."

"Talia..."

"I'm going. Jesus!"

Jesus? That was a new one.

Diane grabbed her keys and got Alex out to the car. She took extra care when securing her into her car seat, but still managed to hurt her some more as she maneuvered her body under the brace and straps. Finally, it was done and she turned.

Talia was just entering the Kovacs's home and Mrs. Kovacs stood at the door, a sour look on her face.

"I'm so sorry, Mrs. Kovacs!" she called. "There's something really wrong with Alex. I'll call you as soon as I can. Thank you so much!" Mrs. Kovacs flapped her hand at her in a "go" motion and closed her screen door. Diane checked Alex one more time before she climbed behind the wheel for the short ride to the hospital.

Alex screamed the whole way.

◆ ◆ ◆

"WHAT THE HELL do you mean, I can't see her right now?" Diane yelled. "She's my daughter and she's in pain! Let me in there!"

Two orderlies held her, one on each arm, as a nurse stood warily in front of her, looking ready to defend herself if Diane broke free.

"I'm sorry, Mrs. Davis—"

"*Ms.* Davis!"

"I can only tell you what I've been instructed to tell you. And that is, once again, that, at least for right now, you cannot see Alex."

"But why? She's my little girl."

The nurse raised her hands, palms out. "Please, ma'am, don't make this any harder than it is. Go take a seat in the waiting room. Frank here will get you a coffee and—"

"I don't want a goddamn coffee!"

"Please, Ms. Davis."

"Ma'am? Mrs. Davis?" Someone behind her was trying to get her attention.

Now who's this? Diane turned as much as she could while still being gripped by the two orderlies.

Cops? What the hell's going on here?

"Could we have a word with you, Mrs. Davis?"

The nurse stepped in. "It's Ms. Davis," she said.

"Thanks," the first officer said. "What do you say, Ms. Davis? Can we grab a coffee and talk?"

"What's with the goddamn coffee? I don't want a coffee!" She struggled between the orderlies. "Do I look like I need a goddamn coffee?"

The officer looked at the nurse. "Is there someplace where we can...?"

"Exam room five is open," she said.

"Thanks." He looked at the orderlies. "We can take it from here."

One orderly raised his eyebrows. When they released Diane she seemed to sag. The second officer took her gently, but firmly, by the elbow and the three of them walked the short distance to the exam room.

"Have a seat," the first officer said, indicating the plastic chair farthest from the door.

"I'd rather stand," Diane said.

"Please," the officer said. "Ms. Davis. Take. A. Seat."

She sat.

"I'm Constable McDonald and this is Constable Sydock."

Normally, Diane would answer with either her name or a "pleased to meet you," but they obviously knew who she was and she wasn't pleased about anything at the moment. Instead, she nodded.

Constable Sydock took the other plastic seat and Constable McDonald leaned against the exam table, crinkling the paper pulled over it.

"What's this about, Constable?" Diane said. "Why won't they let me see Alex?"

"That's what we'd like to talk to you about," McDonald said. "Tell me about Alex. How'd she get hurt?"

Diane told them about Alex being in the high chair, about arguing with Talia about breakfast, and then, out of nowhere, the screaming.

"And where were you when she started to cry?"

"I was standing in front of her. Like I said, I'd just given her a hug. She was asking for another one."

"And your other daughter?" McDonald looked at Sydock, who had a small notebook out and was scribbling in it.

"Talia," Sydock said.

"Your daughter Talia," McDonald continued, "where was she?"

"Standing beside the kitchen table."

"How far away from Alex?"

"Why?"

"How far away, ma'am?"

"Uh...I don't know," she said, looking down, trying to remember. "Three or four feet?"

"And you were facing Alex the entire time?"

"Yes."

"And you can't remember if anything else happened?"

"What do you mean 'anything else'?"

"Anything else," McDonald said. "Anything at all."

Diane started as the memory came back. "Yes!" she said. Sydock sat straighter, pen poised. "I remember hearing a popping noise. Maybe two."

"A popping noise?" Sydock said.

"Yes," she said. "Sort of. Like, I don't know." She swallowed. "Like a cracking noise?"

"A cracking noise?" McDonald said.

"Yeah," she said. "Almost like when you snap a branch over your knee or something."

She saw a look pass between the two cops as McDonald cleared his throat.

"What?" she said.

"What do you think made that noise?" McDonald said.

"I haven't the faintest—well, I assume it was her...arm...breaking," Diane said, her voice fading. Then she rallied herself, and raised her head to look McDonald in the eye. "Look, I've answered all your questions. What's this all about?"

"Ma'am, please," McDonald said. "Bear with me just a bit longer. I want to be sure I've got this exactly straight. You say your daughter Alex was in the high chair, eating cereal. Your other daughter Talia came in, you two did a little back and forth about breakfast, Alex did something cute and you hugged her, you heard a snapping or popping noise, and the next thing you knew, Alex was crying. At no point did you have your head turned away from either of your two daughters. That about right?"

"Yes," Diane said.

"And your daughter Talia is currently where?"

"Next door at the Kovacs's."

"And is there anything else you might want to tell us about what happened this morning with Alex?"

"No."

"Okay," McDonald said and looked over at Sydock. Out of the corner of her eye, she saw Sydock nod. "I think we've got what we came for."

McDonald sighed and stood. "Ms. Davis, could you stand and face the wall, please?"

"I will not! You will tell me what this is about, right now! I want to see Alex! Right now!"

"Ms. Davis, I'm going to ask you one more time to stand, turn, and face the wall. If you do not comply with these instructions, Constable Sydock here will make sure that you do. We can do it easy, or we can do it hard, Ms. Davis. The choice is yours."

Diane knew what was coming. Tears sprang to her eyes and her breath hitched in her chest.

Still, she stood, turned, and faced the wall.

She felt McDonald's calloused hands as he placed the handcuffs first on one wrist then on the other while Sydock said, "Ms. Davis, you are under arrest."

Sydock said a lot more after that, but Diane didn't hear any of it. She was only dimly aware of the wall hitting her face as the world faded to black and she passed out.

CHAPTER SIX
SUMMER 1976

TALIA GOT THE feeling she might have fucked up this time.

The cops showed up at the Kovacs's door sometime after her mother had rushed off with Alex. Talia was told — because Crabby Kovacs never asked — to go down to the rec room and watch TV while they chatted with the police.

Tal didn't like it, but she did it anyway. She turned the TV on, spun the channel dial until she found something worth watching, and then turned the volume up enough to make the adults think that it was safe to talk. After that, she took a walk through their minds.

McDonald, whose first name, unbelievably, was Ronald — which he hated, so he went by his middle name, Ellery, even though he thought it made him sound like a limp-wristed fag — had arrested her mother. There was a dark, hateful fog around her image in his head because he thought she was mistreating Alex. There was the fact that each arm was broken in two places — halfway between shoulder and elbow, and again between elbow and wrist — but there was also Alex's missing front tooth that, to him, was further evidence of child abuse. There was a vague cloud, unfocused but slowly coalescing, around the idea that she somehow might have snapped under the pressure of raising the two girls on her own.

The other cop, Sydock, wasn't quite as convinced Diane — whom he thought of as "the hottie" — did it, but he didn't really know who else might have. His mind was much more a blank mist than McDonald's, and instead of suspicions it was filled with images of her boobs or, in his lingo, her "funbags," and the thought of fucking her was ever present. However, Sydock was aware that he might be going a bit easier on her because she was "so fuckable" so he continued to back his partner up, at least for now.

The cops weren't giving the Kovacs all this information, but between what she'd seen in their heads and the nature of the questions they were asking, Tal got a pretty good idea of what was going on — *Have you heard the kids crying a lot? Have you seen any bruising or other injuries on the children?* — and the Kovacs were putting together a story that fit neatly with McDonald's.

Mr. Kovacs's mind lit up bright yellow as he recalled scraping up Mr. Whiskers from their front step, and Talia felt the confusion, pain, and suspicion he'd been wracked with at the time return. She saw him digging a hole in his backyard, way at the rear of his property where the neatly trimmed grass met the scrubby open fields. She knew he'd dug that hole as a way to delay what he had to do, which was kill the cat to put it out of its misery, but he was conflicted between the desire to be with it a little longer and prolonging its pain. Talia saw him finish the hole, then lean down slowly on one knee — she heard the sharp pop of the knee joint as it bent — to stroke Mr. Whiskers's head one last time. Then the image blurred and Tal didn't know why until she realized it was the tears welling in Mr. Kovacs's eyes that hazed the image of the tortured beast. She saw him clear his vision with the heel of his hand, first his right eye and then his left, before standing and taking a deep breath that seemed to rattle in his chest with a barely-controlled sob. He said, "I love you, Whiskers," but in his head he was thinking, *Make it quick, make it quick, make it quick*, and then he brought the blade of the shovel up, slamming it down

55

quickly, severing the cat's head from its twisted, broken body. After that, there were no real images because Kovacs allowed his grief and the tears it brought with it to overcome him.

Fucking sissy, she thought.

But she saw the way his mind connected that incident with the questions the police were asking, bridging the two events. Hurting the cat, hurting the kids. And she felt a stony hardness settle in him, felt him setting his jaw and clenching his fists.

Shit, she thought. *This isn't good.*

Finally, she jumped over to Crabby Kovacs's mind and let out a squeak of laughter when she discovered that her neighbour's name had been Esther Chopa before she got married. *Good Christ, who'd saddle their poor kid with a handle like that?* she wondered. Esther, Talia soon found out, had been a bit of a wild child herself when she was younger. When she managed to get herself knocked up at the ripe old age of sixteen she'd gone to see a guy who did abortions but, while he did manage to kill the thing growing inside her, he also managed to puncture some vital stuff at the same time. She eventually got herself to a real hospital when she wouldn't stop bleeding, but she never had to worry about getting knocked up again. Talia saw it then. Just like the mass of cells that could have been her child withered and died, so did something in Esther's head. Unlike the aborted fetus that got flushed out of her body, a blackness settled in her mind and made itself at home there. Albert, whom she met two years after her "little difficulty" and married two years after that, knew from the start that they would never have kids and he made his peace with it. But Esther never did. She knew she made his life harder and she just couldn't seem to forget or forgive herself, even after all these years. She loved Albert, Talia felt it, but she seemed a little contemptuous that he put up with all her shit without standing up to her.

Holy fuck, Tal thought. *That's enough of that sentimental bullshit.*

She left Esther's head quickly, but not before realizing that she had told the cops about her mom losing Talia for hours that night she destroyed the squirrel.

Not too long after that, the cops made their way downstairs to talk to her. Sydock sat in a chair opposite the couch she was sitting on, while McDonald went over to the TV and turned the sound down to nothing.

"Hello, Talia," McDonald said. "I'm El and this is John. Can we talk to you for a bit?"

Tal wanted to shout, *Your name's Ronald, you fucking faggot!* but she held back. It wouldn't do any good to throw more fuel on this fire. She'd show her manners and talk like the kid she was supposed to be.

"Sure," she said. "How's Lex?"

"Your sister's going to be fine," McDonald said. "She's going to have to stay in the hospital for a little while, but you'll be able to visit her in a couple of days. How do you get along with Alex?"

I hate the little bitch. She sent my dad away, so how the hell do you think I get along with her? "Fine. Sometimes we fight, but she's cool." She waited what she felt was an appropriate amount of time, then asked, "Where's Mom?"

McDonald smiled. Sydock scribbled notes in his notebook. "How do you two get along with your mother?"

"Good."

"Can you tell me a little more?"

Can you go fuck yourself, Ronny? "Well, she looks after us and she works hard, and that's cuz she loves us." *Christ.* Talking like this made her want to puke. Did she really used to talk like this all the time?

"*Does* she love you?"

Tal didn't miss the emphasis on that first word. Still, she hesitated, thinking of how her mother's face only lit up for Lex now, but decided not to share that particular chestnut. "Yeah," she said.

"You don't seem so sure about that."

"No, it's just I don't really know what you mean."

McDonald laughed a little. She felt him trying to make himself feel more friendly to her. It wasn't working. "I'm sorry," he said. "If you don't understand something, you just go ahead and tell me, okay?"

Tal nodded.

"So, what I meant was, are there times when it feels like maybe she doesn't love you?"

What, like when her brown funk blows away when she concentrates on her other kid instead of me? Fuck yeah. "No sir," she said. "Even if she gets mad, it's only because we did something we weren't supposed to."

"Does she get mad a lot, your mom?"

"No, not really."

"When she is mad, what does she do?"

"Yell and stuff."

"And stuff?"

"Well, sometimes we have to do a timeout in the kitchen, or if Lex and I are fighting, we'll have to go to different rooms."

"That it?"

"Yes sir."

"You have very good manners, Talia." McDonald smiled and she saw the subdued glint of cigarette-yellowed teeth. *The cancer's gonna get you, Ronny.*

"Mom taught us to be respectful of our elders."

"She obviously did a good job. Wouldn't you say?" McDonald said, turning to Sydock. The other cop smiled and nodded, but didn't look up from his notepad.

"Now, you said your mom yells and stuff, but what about this morning?"

"What do you mean?"

58

"Can you tell us what happened this morning?"

Talia told them about just wanting toast, and her mom wanting her to eat more, and about Lex playing with her Cheerios.

"And then what happened?"

"I don't know, sir." Talia frowned. "Lex just started crying. I hate it when she cries, so I just took off outta the kitchen."

"Did you hear anything, or see anything, before she started to cry?"

"Hear anything?"

"Yes, anything. Maybe a bang or a snap?"

Talia made a show of thinking hard. She furrowed her brows. "No sir."

"And where was your mom?"

"She was standing by the table."

"Near your sister?"

"Not really, no."

"You think she could have reached her by just stretching out her arm?" McDonald demonstrated what he meant by reaching for Talia.

"No sir."

"You sure?"

"Yes sir."

McDonald blew some air from his puffed-up cheeks and glanced at his partner. Sydock looked up from his notepad, but his eyes were expressionless.

"Have you seen your dad lately?" McDonald asked.

"No sir," she said. "Not in a long time. Not since Unca...since Uncle Charlie died." *Not since I slowed his heart down and he stared at me, knowing it was me doing it because I was in his head at the same time.* She paused and McDonald let her take her time. "But he calls every so often. Birthdays and stuff."

"Have you talked to him lately?"

"No, it's been a long time."

59

"Do you know where he is?"

"He's got a new job and he travels a lot. I don't know where he is now."

McDonald looked over at Sydock with raised eyebrows. Sydock nodded back.

"Okay, Talia, you've been very helpful today." He leaned down so they were eye to eye. "I've just got a couple more things then we'll leave you alone, okay?"

"'Kay."

"We also need to talk to your mom a lot more, so it's easier if she stays with us. We're trying to get hold of your dad, but if we can't, we'll figure something else out. In the meantime, the Kovacs said they would let you stay here." He stopped and she knew it was to let all that sink in. "How do you feel about that?"

"Is Lex coming here too?"

"Maybe, but not for a few days. Hopefully your dad will be here by then."

"Can I maybe go home and get some stuff? Clothes and things?"

"Of course!" McDonald said, a big fake smile creasing his face. "That's one of the good things about being right next door, right?"

"When will Mom be home?"

"I'm not sure, Talia."

"So it could be a while?" She waited and got the answer she was looking for. McDonald's mind darkened as he thought, *It'll be a cold fucking day in hell before I let that child-beating bitch go.*

"I don't really know, Talia. That's as honest an answer as I can give you." He was jonesing for a cigarette, she could feel it. Time to wrap this up.

"Okay."

"You sure you're okay with all this?"

"Well, no, not really. I'd rather be home with Mom, but I guess if I have to…"

"You do for now."

"Okay."

"Okay," McDonald said as he slapped his palms on his thighs and rose from his seat. "I want to thank you again for talking with us, Talia. Any time you want to talk, you just tell Mr. or Mrs. Kovacs and they'll let me know, okay?"

"Sure," she said. *Yeah, you'd like some information so you can lock up Mom even longer, wouldn't you? Meanwhile, your partner's thinking about getting his dick wet with her. Great team you are.* Despite her thoughts, she kept her expression neutral, but it was getting harder.

Thankfully, with that, they went back upstairs, talked again briefly with the Kovacs, and then they left. She felt the sweet rush of cigarette smoke fill McDonald's blackened lungs before he even got to the car.

And then she was stuck with the motherfucking Kovacs.

Yup, I fucked up this time.

CHAPTER SEVEN
SUMMER 1976

AFTER THE COPS left, the Kovacs made a late lunch that Talia only picked at. It was sandwiches, that much she recognized, but the bread wasn't white and the meat was all weird-looking and spicy and it smelled funny. Mr. Kovacs asked her if she liked cheese and she said yes, and was rewarded with some unidentifiable white stuff. This wasn't the cheese slices she was used to. They didn't even have any Cheez Whiz!

Maybe when they took her over to her own place she could sneak some real food back. She was going to die if she had to eat this shit for too long. In the meantime, Mrs. Kovacs tut-tutted over her not eating, but Mr. Kovacs came to the rescue when he told his wife to go easy on her, because she was probably lonely with both her mom and sister gone.

Crabby Kovacs took her plate away. "Well, she doesn't have to play with it. I'll wrap it up and she can have it for lunch tomorrow."

Talia bit back the retort that jumped to her lips.

After cleaning up, they walked next door to Talia's house and picked up her clothes and toiletries.

"Do you want to bring some games or something?" Mr. Kovacs asked.

"Can I bring a book?"

"Sure you can, bring a few."

She brought just one. The Book.

Oh, she thought, *the thinks I'm going to fucking think.*

At least now she had a friend. Even just holding It as she pulled It from the shelf to put in her bag made her feel immediately better. She knew the food wouldn't be a problem anymore. The Book would fix that. So she didn't even bother trying to sneak food over.

She couldn't have anyway, with that fat bitch bird-dogging her every goddamn step.

Yeah, some things were going to change. And Talia was going to start with Mrs. Kovacs.

CHAPTER EIGHT
FALL 1976

SUMMER ENDED. JERRY Lewis had a telethon that Mrs. Kovacs watched religiously every year, always donating twenty-five dollars to the cause. Talia knew this because she went on and on about "those poor Jerry's kids."

To Talia, Jerry Lewis was the man that always put the final nail in the coffin of summer. Him and his fucking kids.

School started and there was still the Spooky Talia name-calling. But this year, there was more of it. There was also the added gossip about how her mother was a child-beater and her father was nowhere to be found.

Tal took some pleasure from all the tripping and walking headlong into lockers, walls, and doors that happened around her. It didn't shut anyone up, but it sure as hell put a smile on her face.

From what Talia understood, Alex was healing, and probably could have come home by now, but with no parents around it made more sense to just keep her in the hospital.

So they were both prisoners at this point.

Talia had been holding back on her experiments lately; the last time she really let loose, she kind of fucked herself over so she was waiting a bit, choosing her moment. Choosing her battles, as her mother would say. But that got harder and harder as time passed. Mr. Kovacs was bad enough, still ruminating over his dead cat and what Tal's mom might have done to it. Eventually he started to look at Talia and wonder about her as well.

She distinctly heard the same phrase play over and over in the back of his mind when he looked at her. *The apple doesn't fall far from the tree. Nope, the apple does not fall far from the tree.*

So there was all that bullshit going on. But then there was Mrs. Kovacs. Good old Esther. She was a goddamn psychopath.

She made Talia have a shower every morning *and* evening—like she was going to get dirty just going to bed—and she had to wash her hands pretty much every time she touched anything. This coming from the same woman who finished her dinner and then put her plate down on the floor for her fat-assed dog to slurp up the leavings. "Dogs' mouths are cleaner than ours, you know," she once said when she caught Tal staring open-mouthed at her. Tal didn't know if that was true, but she still thought Esther was a hypocrite, and a mean one at that.

That day the cops came was the one and only time Talia was given free rein of the shows she could watch on TV. Damn near anything she wanted to watch Mrs. Kovacs considered "juvenile" or "inappropriate for young ladies." In fact, news and documentaries seemed to be the only things that Crabby Kovacs approved of and, since she had no interest in either, TV was out.

Bedtime was a sore spot as well. At home, she went to bed around nine-thirty, and that was usually after some sort of wrestling or pillow fight with Lex or her mom and a last drink of milk or water.

Her new guardians felt that young minds should be in bed by eight-thirty. "Early to bed and early to rise," Mrs. Kovacs always said. And no drinks before bed either, because old Fat-Ass thought she might piss herself in her sleep.

It became unbearable. All the rules, all the showers, all the changes to her life.

Finally, when Crabby Kovacs sent her to bed at eight-thirty on a Friday night, Talia decided she'd had enough. This was it, the end of the line.

While the old bitch was preoccupied, Talia went to work.

Normally, Fat-Ass Esther's fat-ass dog wouldn't leave her side. This was mostly because the nasty bitch was always dropping little snacks or scraps of food — *no wonder both their asses are as big as double-wide trailers* — so the mongrel followed her like its life depended on it.

Yeah, well, not tonight, Talia thought. Tonight, Benji's life was in Talia's hands.

Talia sat on her bed and reached out with her mind until she found the blissfully simple thoughts of the dog. As usual, it lay by Mrs. Kovacs as she watched TV. Benji dozed, snoring slightly. She caught a glimpse in its mind of the cat, Mr. Whiskers. The thing was dreaming of the cat. How cute. How adorable.

She squashed the dream, roused the dog, and brought him upstairs. He wasn't happy about it and fought her, but she had control now. Control enough that she could not only get the fat fuck up the stairs, but do it so quietly that the Kovacs didn't even notice.

Benji eventually rounded the corner and stepped into her room. The dog looked at her warily and, for a second, Talia experienced a weird doubling of her seeing the dog as the dog saw her. The dog radiated reluctance and dislike for her. Not that she gave a shit; she felt the same way about it.

She ordered it up onto the bed. It slowly walked over and made an effort to get its front paws onto the mattress, but beyond that, it seemed completely incapable of hauling its ass the rest of the way up.

And it didn't want to. It still carried puppy memories of the beatings it had endured when it jumped on any of the furniture, with the sole exception of Esther's side of the bed.

And even she was too lazy to pick him up. She got Albert to do it.

Talia reached out, stilled the thing's mental rebellion, and then pushed again from inside her head. The dog rose from the floor and she felt its fear and confusion. She wrapped an enclosure of comfort around its mind and slowed its heartbeat. Wouldn't do to have the damn thing panic now and ruin her plans.

Then Benji was on the bed. It stood shaking, waiting for the beating. She reached out and stroked the dog's head. *No beating. No beating.*

It wanted to bite her. It wanted down. It wanted to go back to Mrs. Kovacs where it was safe. *Bite. Down. Bite. Down. Bite bite bite!* Its thoughts spun in a furious loop inside its head.

It would do none of that. Talia wouldn't let it.

She opened the dog's mouth, which wasn't hard. It was on the edge of panic, but still pliable. The thing was gonna die, but she needed a tooth first. And his were bigger than the other two.

That seemed to be a problem.

She wrapped her fingers around the top fang, braced her thumb securely against it and pulled. Then she pulled harder. The dog's head angled with each tug, but the tooth wouldn't budge. Benji was riding into full-blown panic now.

She reached inside his head and tried to soothe him but it didn't seem to help. His eyes rolled back, his tongue dangled, foamy with saliva as he huffed out desperate pants. His ears and tail twitched frantically.

And through it all — *bite bite BITE!*

She let go of the tooth but didn't relax her concentration. Not even a little. She knew what happened when she did that. No way was she getting bitten again.

Instead, she opened her hand and placed it palm up under the tooth. Then, keeping everything else under control while also ensuring the dog didn't move, she focused on the tooth. She saw it with her mind, saw the way the gum sheathed it and then, reaching out mentally instead of with her fingers, she *pulled*.

The tooth dropped into her hand along with a hot gout of blood.

She held the entire tooth, root and all. She was ecstatic with the results, but not so crazy about the blood. She reached out one more time and pinched off all the open blood vessels in the dog's mouth. It whimpered, eyes rolling back completely, and went limp.

Holy fuck, she thought. *I made him pass out! Cool!*

Next, all the blood had to go away. So, she made it go away. One second it was there, then, with no palpable passing of time, it was gone.

Now the dog.

She had myriad ways to kill it. She hesitated as she considered her options.

And hesitated some more.

Dammit. She finally had to admit to herself that she didn't really want to kill him.

But she did! If only to get back at that bitch, Esther.

That's the problem, she thought. *It's Crabby Kovacs I want to hurt, not her stupid fat-assed dog.* Yes, she had to admit she didn't like the thing. It was ugly and stupid. But it couldn't help the ugly, and the stupid came from how it was raised. Again, that was Crabby Kovacs's fault. Not the dog's.

But it went deeper than that.

Unca Charlie wanted to do bad things with her.

Mr. Squirrel had been mean. He'd bitten her.

Mr. Whiskers had turned on her and attacked her.

Hell, even Lex was annoying and turned both her dad and her mom against her.

But what had the dog done, besides just be a dog?

She still wanted to punish Mrs. Kovacs, so she sent the damned dog away, just like the blood. One second he was on the bed, the next, the slight depression in the bedclothes rose back to normal with no weight to hold them down anymore.

Isn't that just like killing him though? she wondered. She had to admit it was.

"God *damn* it." Talia said, but quietly. The Kovacs were still downstairs, still watching TV, still unaware the dog was missing. But they also seemed to, at the most inappropriate times, have superhero hearing. So she kept her voice low.

She called the dog back again. How she did it, she didn't know. She just reached out and found him. She didn't even know where she was reaching out to. Not any place on Earth, that's for sure. There was no map for wherever that dog was. But she could reach out and find him. He had her...her distinction on him. Like he'd been...what? *Tagged? Marked?* She didn't know. But he stood out as somehow *hers.* So, she brought Benji back.

Or what was left of him.

He looked no different. Still missing a tooth. Conscious again, which was good. She didn't know how she would have explained an unconscious dog on her bed.

So, outwardly, not much difference. But he *was* different. She could tell. He stood, unsteadily, but under his own power, and jumped—more like fell—off the bed, stumbled, then picked himself up clumsily and slowly walked to the door of her bedroom. Once there, he looked left, as though he wanted to get back downstairs to his master, but instead he turned right and headed down the hall toward the Kovacs's bedroom.

Talia heard him settle, could picture him curling into a fat ball at the foot of their bed, shifting a little to get comfortable, then, with an exhalation that was as much a groan as a sigh, close his eyes.

She climbed into bed and did much the same thing. Sleep took her quickly.

♦ ♦ ♦

"OH MY LORD!"

Talia woke to the screeching of a banshee. The wailing was of a pitch designed to shatter wine glasses and destroy equilibrium through the annihilation of eardrums. Her eardrums in particular.

She sat up. Darkness sucked everything out of the room, save the shrieking of Esther. *What the hell?*

"What's the matter with my baby? Oh, my poor, poor baby!"

Details filled in as her eyes adapted to the darkness and her mind cleared away the muzziness of sleep. The first detail to make an impact was the smell—horrible, eye-watering.

Shit.

She threw back the covers and slid out of bed. Carefully, she moved to the door, though she needn't have worried about making any noise. Esther was the Olympic champion in that area right now.

She came hurtling down the hall like an unstoppable freight train to meet Talia at the door. Talia narrowly missed bouncing off her chest.

"What did you do to him?" Her voice was a bullhorn.

"What?" Talia was still trying to put this together logically. She was failing miserably. "What?" she asked again, stupidly.

"BEN. JEE." The name was two shotgun blasts from her mouth. "What did you do to him?" Then, with no warning, her finger came up into Talia's face and her voice got low and sinister. "You fed him something, didn't you?"

"Fed? What? No!"

"I don't believe you!" Back to bullhorn. "You did! You fed my baby something! And now..." Her voice broke. "And now..."

The tears started then, and that was worse than the bullhorn, worse than the low sinister voice, and worse than the finger in her face.

And underneath it all, creeping into Talia's mind, a greyish-purple fog from Esther's scrambled brain: *dirty girl dirty dirty girl whore for a mom animal killer dirty dirty dirty girl.*

Talia took a step back, not from fright, not from surprise, but from indignation. *Dirty girl? Really? Strong words coming from the coat-hanger abortion queen.*

Esther seemed to sense some sort of victory, or admission of guilt, and took a step forward, both hands coming up, clenched into claws.

Then Albert came down the hall, his hands out in a placating gesture. "Now Mum, you calm down." His nose wrinkled at the smell. "Talia, you go on back to bed. There's nothing that can't be talked over in the morning."

Talia looked at him uncertainly. Esther's face seemed to cycle through various shades of red, but she held her tongue. Mr. Kovacs tilted his head at Talia, gesturing her back into her room.

Talia turned on her heel and walked back to the bed. With one last glance at the two of them, she climbed beneath the covers and pulled them up tight.

Albert dragged his seething wife away from the door. "Now, what in the blue hell's going on, Mum?" he said. Tal couldn't make out the answer, buried as it was in the sobs emanating from her constricted throat.

Instead, she walked through their minds. Well, his anyway. Esther's was a confused hurricane of fragmented thoughts. She was able to pick out only words—baby, poop, mess, dirty, smell, sick...

His were easier and, from them, Tal could work out what they were doing and saying.

What they were doing was cleaning up the shit and vomit that the dog had blown all over their room. Through Albert's eyes, Talia saw the light- and dark-brown pools—far more than reasonably could have come from a dog, even one as fat as Benji—spattered seemingly everywhere. Puddles and runnels, like liquid land mines, covered the majority of the floor space. Talia didn't focus too much on the cleanup as every time Mr. Kovacs gagged—which was quite often—she would too. So instead of the walk she normally took, she gingerly danced over the surface of his brain like a water spider. She didn't get anywhere near as much information that way, but it was still useful for picking up impressions.

What it came down to was that Albert was trying to be rational about the whole thing, but Talia knew he now wanted her out as badly as Esther did. She knew he would work to finalize something tomorrow. And then she glimpsed a brief skittering of thought that excited her.

They'd found Glen.

They'd found her dad.

CHAPTER NINE
WINTER 1976

THEY'D LOCATED GLEN, but it took another week to contact him and a couple more for him to move some stuff around in his schedule so that he could move back into his former home in New Hope. By then, Halloween had come and gone, and the snow had begun to pile up.

Those last three weeks in the Kovacs's home were strained, but quiet. Benji was put down a couple of days after the incident. Even though the vet had told the Kovacs it was nothing the dog had been fed, more that he was just getting old and overweight, Crabby Kovacs didn't lighten up on Talia. Within a couple of days she'd stopped talking to her altogether, leaving all communication to Mr. Kovacs.

When she wasn't being ignored at school, Talia spent a lot of time in her room with the Book, being ignored by the Kovacs. The only upside was that she no longer had to have a shower twice a day. Esther wouldn't talk to her to enforce it, and Mr. Kovacs was picking his battles.

The uneasy truce lasted until her dad parked his pathetic Volkswagen Beetle in their driveway.

Talia was turned over to his custody with barely restrained enthusiasm. Mrs. Kovacs stayed in the kitchen, perched on the edge of one of the chairs, hands knotted as though in prayer that Glen wouldn't tell them it was all some mistake, that he was just coming to let them know Tal was, in fact, staying with them.

If that was the case, her prayers were answered. Glen thanked Mr. Kovacs, shook his hand, accepted the cardboard box of Talia's belongings, and headed back over to their house. If he noticed the slightly sour, yet still somehow gleeful look on Mr. Kovacs's face, he didn't react.

Instead, Glen wrapped his daughter up in a big bear hug that lasted a long time. Talia didn't care, she would have been happy if it had gone on forever.

Her father was home!

When Talia and her dad got to the door of their house, they stood on the front steps for a moment as he fumbled with the box of her belongings while trying to free up a hand to reach for his keys. "Hey Poopypants, wanna do your old man a solid?"

Talia looked up at him, uncomprehending.

He smirked. "Can you reach into my pocket and get out the keys?" He thrust a hip toward her. "I kinda got my hands full here, ya know?"

Talia reached, paused, and then reached again. Her hand slid into the pocket of his jeans. She didn't want to put her hand all the way in, but she could feel nothing except cloth.

"Gotta dig a little deeper than that, kiddo," he said. "Come on, this box ain't light. What the heck you got in here?"

"A book and stuff," she said. She pushed lower and felt the hard points of the keys. She caught a couple of them between her fingers, pulled up, then got a better grip on them and pulled them out. They jingled merrily as they broke past the seam of the pocket.

"There ya go," Glen said. "You wanna do the honours?" He nodded toward the lock.

Talia unlocked the door and stepped inside. Her father followed behind her, dropping the box in the entranceway and stooping to brush the clinging snow off his boots. "Cold in here," he said. "Must have turned the heat down while your mom is…not around." He cleared his throat, a little uncomfortably, Talia thought, but let it slide. She was just glad to be out from under the Kovacs' rule. "Let's see what we can do about getting some heat going here," he said. "You may need a sweater for a couple of hours though, kiddo."

She nodded and grabbed the edge of the box to drag it into her room. "Want some help with that?" Glen asked.

"Nah, I'm good." She trusted him, but really didn't want him digging around in her stuff. She didn't need him looking at the Book. Maybe she'd tell him about it a little later.

"Okay, go get squared away while I check out the food situation—" Talia had completely forgotten how he pronounced that last word—*sit-chee-ay-shun*—and burst into laughter. She couldn't remember the last time she had laughed. For the first time in a long time, she felt *good*. Optimistic.

She grabbed the box and bumped her way down the hall. She heard her father as he took stock of the kitchen. "Everything looks pretty much the same. Looks like your mom didn't change much on me, did she, Poopypants?"

Ten minutes later, they were back in the car.

She looked over at her father and her heart swelled. It felt as if it would burst from her chest. She still couldn't quite believe it. Dad was home.

Maybe things could get back to normal now. Maybe she could even think about getting rid of the Book.

A half-hour later, they were loaded up with groceries. Talia was shocked at how fast he went through the store. Mom always agonized over which dish soap to buy for hours. Not Dad. He was more of a grab-and-go kind of shopper. She liked that.

Then they were at the hospital. Talia liked coming here, despite the fact that the visits were always because someone was sick or hurt. It wasn't the hospital itself, but the view behind it. The building was nestled in the embrace of a curved-out section of a small mountain. The sharp, bright angles of the hospital contrasted with the soft angles of the wall of rock that rose behind it. She liked to imagine herself climbing that mountain someday.

At least if I fell, I wouldn't be far from help, she thought. Then she thought, *The apple doesn't fall far from the tree.* It lingered only a moment before she shoved it aside.

She took one last look at the mountain and the pine trees that peppered its grey expanse with green before they entered the hospital.

It seemed to take forever to get Lex out. Her father had to sign forms, show identification and other papers, and talk to person after person, some in medical garb, some in suits.

Talia did what she could to stay calm. It was tough, but she did it.

Finally, they were allowed in to see her sister and Talia was stunned. It had only been a few weeks, but still, Lex had *grown!* She seemed to have gone from eighteen months to five years old overnight. It was crazy! She still had full casts on both her arms, from shoulder to wrist, but her hands seemed to be free and useful.

As shocking as it was for Talia, it seemed to be a million times more so for her dad. He hadn't seen Lex in almost two years. He stopped at the door, taking her in, casts and all. Then he dropped to one knee and stretched out his arms to her.

Lex hung back, chewing on her lower lip. Talia stood beside her dad, waiting.

Lex wasn't moving. She stood, swaying her body from side to side.

"Lex!" Talia said. Her younger sister looked at her. "It's okay, Lex," she said. "It's Daddy. He came home."

She looked to her father. He hadn't moved, giving her the time she needed.

"Daddy?" she said.

"Yeah, honey," Glen said. "It's me."

And Lex ran to him. Then they were both crying.

Talia even felt herself tearing up a bit, but she fought it back.

Her father was instructed on how to care for Alex and given a schedule for regular checkups. From what Tal could tell, Lex would get the lower casts off a bit sooner, but the upper arms needed longer to heal.

Great, Talia thought. *Everyone will be fussing over her and I'll have to do all the work, like usual. Shoulda broken her skull.*

By the time they got back home, it was dinnertime.

"Nothing fancy tonight, guys," Dad said. "How's wienies and beans sound?" It didn't sound great, but Talia loved it anyway. It wasn't so much the food as it was her father's rendition of the *Beans, Beans, the Musical Fruit* song, complete with a protracted fart at the end.

Lex laughed so hard that she started to choke, until her father thumped her on the back.

After dinner, he sent the two of them off to get reacquainted while he cleaned up. That proved to be a pleasant surprise for Talia. She'd figured she'd be targeted for dish duty while Dad played with Lex.

In the end, as it turned out, she would have rather done the dishes. Alex and Talia found themselves sitting at opposite ends of the ugly brown couch, trading uneasy glances. Lex sucked at her lower lip. Talia picked at the fibres of the couch. They listened to the sounds of their father cleaning up.

I can't stand you, Talia thought. *He's back because of me. He's back in* spite *of you.*

Eventually, Lex announced that she "gotta go bat'room" and ran into the kitchen. Talia heard her asking Dad for help. When he told her to get Talia to help, she said something that Talia couldn't quite catch. But one word sounded like "creepy." Probably was.

Talia didn't give a shit.

The rest of the evening passed quietly and uneventfully. The three of them sat around watching television until it was time for bed.

◆ ◆ ◆

IT DIDN'T TAKE long to settle into a groove.

Get up, get breakfast, get dressed, get to school, go into a coma, come home, eat, pretend to hang with Lex, watch TV for a while, go to bed, get up and do it all over again.

During that time, Talia learned not to ask about her mom. Lex, however, never seemed to notice the uncomfortable way the air seemed to thicken whenever Dad had to field questions about their mother, so she kept asking them. When she did, Talia left the room.

Even with her father back, Talia found that life still kind of sucked, but at least it sucked less than it had when she was living with the Kovacs.

◆ ◆ ◆

THEN CAME FRIDAY.

It started the same as every other day. Breakfast, dress, school, coma — the full routine.

Friday night, there was a slight break in the monotony. No school the next day, so they were allowed to stay up until eleven. Talia watched some dopey movie about a bulldozer that runs up against a strange bluish meteor and turns into a killer. It was a movie her mother would never have let her watch. Marcia wouldn't have either. She supposed it was a horror movie, but it didn't scare her.

She heard her sister crying while Dad bathed her, but that was standard practice now that she had those stupid casts on her. She was pretty much useless doing anything on her own.

78

Talia was just glad her father wasn't asking her to wipe Lex's ass every time she took a shit.

When they came out, Lex was wrapped in one towel and had another around her head like she was an Arab or something. Her eyes were red-rimmed. "Your dad still hasn't got the trick of keeping the shampoo out of Lex's eyes yet," Dad said. Lex's fingers twitched as though she wanted to rub her eyes, but she couldn't, of course.

Tal knew better than to jump into Lex's head. If her eyes were stinging that would just add to the calliope ride of images in her brain. *Fuck that noise.*

Instead, she turned back to the television as indifferently as she could, banishing the girl from her mind. Dad could fight to get her into her nightclothes all on his own. Talia was staying right here on the couch.

When it was finally time for bed, Tal got up and headed down the hall to the bathroom. She left Dad dozing in his old easy chair, a newspaper draped across his lap.

She was just finishing her pee, balling the toilet paper up in her hand, when the door creaked open a few inches. "I'm in here!" she yelped, pinching her knees together and hunching forward.

"Everything okay, Poopypants?" her father asked.

"Yes! I'm fine! Close the door, Dad!"

"Okay, okay," he said, his face still visible in the slice of space. "I just woke up and you weren't there and the TV was on and—"

"I'm fine," Talia said. It was a struggle to keep her voice even, to keep a lid on things. "Please shut the door. I'll talk to you when I get out."

"Okay." The door started to shut, then slid back open an inch. "Sorry," he said. Another beat and then the door closed for good. She still gave it a count of twenty before she wiped, pulled up her pants, and washed her hands.

When she emerged, her father was back in his chair, the television was still on, and the paper was back on his lap.

"Hey, kiddo," he said. "Sorry 'bout that."

"S'okay," she said, not meaning it.

"Goin' to bed?"

"Yeah."

"'Kay. I'll give you a few minutes, then come in and kiss you goodnight."

"Okay."

"And I promise to knock first, to make sure you're decent." He smiled, and she couldn't help but smile, just a little, back at him.

"Okay," she said.

As it turned out, he gave her lots of time, maybe a half-hour. Long enough that she thought she may need to go out and wake him up again. Even though she had finished changing quite a while ago, and had opened the door, he remained true to his word and rapped lightly on the doorframe before peeking.

She giggled.

Lex hadn't stirred while Talia was changing, or even when her father had knocked. When he entered the room, however, she moaned and fluttered her ineffectual arms with a great flourish of blankets and limbs. Dad paused to watch her, but there was no further movement. He looked over at Talia, shrugged, and moved toward her bed.

She was still smiling, right up until her father's big left hand came down over her mouth.

Then nothing was funny anymore.

Her father raised his right hand up, his index finger pointing as he brought it to his lips. "Shhhhhhh..."

Then the same hand came down and gently pulled at the covers. She felt them sweeping down her body, warm air replaced by cooler air, her skin pimpling in the cold. With a final flick of his wrist, her father sent the duvet plummeting to the floor at the foot of her bed.

And in her mind, there was only an echoing *no no no no no no no no no no...*

She felt his knuckles graze her shin as he gathered her nightgown up in a fist. Then it began to rise up her legs. She willed herself to become heavy, to become stone, so that the fabric would get trapped under her and refuse to give in to his insistent tugging.

For a few moments, it seemed to work.

This is my dad! Maybe he's finally realizing what he's doing is wrong wrong wrong!

Then the tugging got rougher.

There was another voice in her head, but this one was coming from a great distance away. She couldn't make it out over the constant *no no no no no no no no no no no no* encircling her brain.

And still her nightgown rose higher and higher. Baring her knees, then her thighs, then her underpants. She glanced up at her father, the constant pressure of his hand a tight band across her jaw.

What she saw shocked her. His face was shiny with sweat. His mouth hung open, panting. He was panting like Mr. Whiskers had panted at the very end.

~*...Miiiisssssterrrr Whisssskerrrrssss...yyyyessss...*~

And just like that, that far-off voice was in her ear, up close and defending her. The Book.

Of course it was the Book.

How could she have forgotten the Book?

It galvanized her.

She leapt into her sister's mind, quieter now that it was in the throes of sleep. In a slice of a second, she saw the real reason Lex had been crying during her bath.

~*...whyyyy doooo yyyyoooouuuu thiiiinnnnk hhhheeee leeeefffft iiiinnnn theeee fiiiirrrrsssst plaaaacccce? hhhheeee cooooouldnnnn't ssssstooooop hhhhimmmmmseeeelllffff...*~

She stared at her father accusingly.

And looking into his eyes, she knew it was the truth.

~...*yoooourrrr*   *mmmmoooommmm'ssss*   *innnn jaaaaillll...annnnd*   *thissss*   *ffffuckerrrrssss*   *onnnn*   *theeee looooosssse...*~

But it was her father!

~...*deeeearrrr oooold daaaad...*~

And that just wasn't right.

Yeah, she'd fucked up. Yeah, she'd done some shitty things. But there were all these assholes out in the world. Just out there, walking around.

Faces slid across her vision.

Sydock.

Esther.

Others.

But worst of all.

Dad.

Daddy.

My *daddy.*

Talia felt something break inside of her. Nothing physical, but something tactile just the same. It was a sharp snap, just behind her breastbone.

Just about where her father had gotten her nightgown up to.

Suddenly, she had a new mantra in her mind.

No more.

...*no more no more no more no more no more*...

They had to go away. She closed her eyes.

Every one of them.

They all had to just...

♦ ♦ ♦

GO. AWAY.

♦ ♦ ♦

MCDONALD AND SYDOCK pulled out of the diner where they'd stopped for some fresh coffee. It had been a long fucking night already. Friday night, full moon. Didn't get any better than that.

McDonald wanted a few minutes away from the madness of the shift to just enjoy his hot beverage, so he'd pulled rank and told Sydock to take the wheel. Besides, if he drove too long, he got an ache in his shoulders.

They'd just left New Hope proper and were rounding a curve cut out of a massive rock face—the solid stone wall still showed the vertical boreholes where it had been drilled and dynamited to create the opening for the highway—when Sydock made a small noise.

McDonald had been watching the road as he normally did, even while riding in the passenger seat. Two sets of eyes were always better than one, and as much as he would never admit it to his partner, he never trusted anyone else to drive as much as he trusted himself. The way he saw it, unless he was behind the wheel, his life was in someone else's hands.

When he heard the noise he turned. He saw Sydock in the driver's seat, his left hand on the steering wheel, his right holding the Styrofoam cup of coffee inches from his lips. His eyes were wide.

Reflexively, McDonald checked the road ahead of him. Nothing out of the ordinary.

But when his gaze returned to his partner, Sydock was gone. Just…gone. McDonald watched the Styrofoam cup fall to the empty seat, splashing brown liquid across the car's interior before tumbling to the floor.

He reached for the wheel, knowing if he didn't, the car would slam into the rock cut; his training kicked in before his mind could question the logic of what he'd just seen.

His hand never made it to the steering wheel though, as McDonald, too, vanished from the vehicle.

♦ ♦ ♦

ESTHER KOVACS LAY on her side in bed, covers pulled tight under her chin. Her husband of almost forty years lay sprawled on his back beside her, his jaw slack, snoring lightly, but not unpleasantly.

Tears leaked from her eyes. She missed her dog something fierce. It had been almost a month, but she still mourned his death. He'd been such a good boy and somehow that dirty little girl had made him sick.

She tried to keep her sniffling to a minimum, not wanting to wake her husband. She pulled a tissue loose from the box on her night table and dabbed her nose and eyes.

There was a shifting in the bed, which her mind first took as Benji jumping up to join them. But no, that wasn't it.

The snoring was gone.

Her eyes flicked over to her husband's side of the bed just in time to see the covers slowly settling back down onto the mattress, as though they had been fluffed up.

But she hadn't done so.

Has Albert fallen out of bed? she wondered

The first stage of panic was just rocketing into her brain and flooding her body with adrenalin when she evaporated from under the covers as well, leaving only a dampened tissue and some body heat behind.

♦ ♦ ♦

DIANE SAT ON the edge of her thin jail-cell mattress in the dark.

Try as she might, she couldn't sleep—her mind lost to an endless swirling pit of confusion, self-doubt, and regret.

Though there was a voice deep down inside her that said there was no way she could have done what they were saying she had done to Alex, there was another voice, a voice that grew stronger each day, a voice that metastasized like a cancer in her brain, that said that maybe, just maybe, she was somehow responsible for the injuries her daughter sustained.

But how?

Alex. Talia. My little girls. How are they holding up? she wondered. *What is going on with them? Has Glen come home? And is what he was scared of...is it real? Could he really have those urges with his own daughters?*

Her daughters. Talia had seemed to be growing more distant every day. And now

Could Talia have—? *No*, Diane dismissed it out of hand. *There's no way.*

She'd been trying to write her girls a letter. She didn't even know if they'd get it, if that was allowed, but she thought, if nothing else, it might have made her feel better. But she never got past the opening. How could she condense everything she wanted to tell them, everything she felt for them, into a few words on paper?

She felt daunted and became despondent every time she tried.

With no warning, Diane felt a strange curdling sensation in her belly and her vision dimmed.

Then, she was gone.

The pencil bounced off the mattress and clicked onto the concrete floor. The paper followed.

◆ ◆ ◆

MARCIA HAD *To Kill a Mockingbird* propped up against a small mountain of pillows on her bed so that she wouldn't have to hold the book while reading.

She wondered how nerdy she was, getting into a book that was supposed to be for school, but she found herself getting caught up in the story nonetheless.

Besides, it helped take her mind off Talia, Alex, and their poor mom. Marcia knew there had to be some logical explanation as to how Lex's arms were broken, but she also knew that there was no way Ms. D could ever have done that to either one of her girls. Marcia knew her, maybe better than anyone.

She'd even told the police that, but she could tell they didn't believe she knew Ms. D — Diane — as well as she said she did.

What did they —

...oh...

Marcia felt a tingling in her stomach. It quickly turned into something much worse. She had no time to make it to the bathroom. She leaned over the edge of her bed and vomited.

As she did, she felt everything grey out for the briefest of moments.

Then, as quickly as the nausea had come, it was gone again. The taste of sick was still on her tongue, but she felt fine. Better than fine actually.

She felt as though she'd just dodged something monstrous and horrible and was now wrapped in loving, comforting arms.

She felt safe.

What was that all about? she wondered.

♦ ♦ ♦

TALIA'S EYES SNAPPED open. Dad's hand was still over her mouth. He was still panting and sweating.

She made him go away.

There was a slight *pop* that she now knew was the air rushing in to fill the dad-shaped space that had just been vacated.

Then she brought him back.

To Talia, it almost seemed as though someone had changed the channel on her father. He'd been red-faced, sweat-shiny, with a fierce glow of anticipation in his eyes. Then, she'd sent him away. When he came back, he was a whole different version of Dad. Not really Dad anymore. Now he was just another asshole. Glen, the asshole. Face slack, eyes deadened, skin greyish and seemingly older.

She did it again. *Pop.*

Then she did it again.

Then again.

By the time she grew bored of doing it, Glen was a heap on the floor, his hair patched with white in the few places it hadn't come out altogether. Some of his teeth were missing, he was bleeding from his ears and nose, and there was even blood dripping like tears from his eyes. The air was fouled with the smell of shit and piss. Vomit stained the front of his shirt and pants.

But the part Talia liked the best was the chunks that had been taken out of him. Clawed out or bitten off, she didn't care. It was just as funny either way.

The fucker.

She listened to the bubbling, keening sound that came from Glen for quite a while before she noticed something else.

A jumbled sharpness in her hand.

Looking down, she opened her clenched fist. Teeth.

Seven of them.

Seven?

She counted again. Definitely seven.

Sydock. McDonald. The Kovacs. Mom. Glen.

Oh god. Marcia?

That's when she looked over at her sister's bed.

No Lex.

Huh.

She didn't remember sending her away. She remembered all the faces flashing past her mind's eye, remembered pulling back on one, Marcia's. She didn't remember Lex's at all.

~...shhhheeee issss allllreadyyyy oooouuuurrrrssss...~

Huh?

It didn't really bother her too much. While she hadn't intended on making Lex go away, she sure as hell wasn't broken up about it.

It was no big deal.

And it had added another tooth to her collection. That was a bonus, wasn't it?

Maybe I can keep adding to it, she thought.

By then, the Glen-thing was getting on her nerves. She disappeared him one last time—blood, puke, and all—and went to bed.

She slept soundly.

And the next day, she watched television all day long and ate whatever she wanted.

EPILOGUE
WINTER 1981

TALIA WATCHED AS the nerd squad — Theo, the Toad, Stash, and Crouch — passed by her in the hall. She looked in the direction they were going. Sure enough, there was Steph. The four of them — well, okay, Theo, Stash, and the Toad — followed her around like lost puppies. Crouch just followed the other three. His interests seemed to veer more toward her old babysitter Marcia, and alcoholic stupors.

Talia reached into her sweater pocket, her hand sliding into the comforting, clicking hardness of the teeth there. Teeth of all shapes and sizes. Some from animals, but most from humans. She loved to run her fingers through them, feel them part like giant grains of sand.

Then the voice started up.

~...*ssssoooonnnnn yyyyooooouuuu'llll haaaavvvve toooo mmmmake doooo wiiiith wwwwhaaaat yyyyooooouuuu haaaavvvve*...~

That voice used to be such a comfort to her, just like the teeth. But now It seemed more like a nagging parent.

Still, It was the only parent she'd really had in the past few years. She'd been bounced from foster home to foster home, never seeming to last long in any of them.

Not that she gave a shit. It just got her more teeth.

When her aunt and uncle moved to town, Talia had no interest in living with them as they'd planned. Hell, she even got rid of her uncle, figuring Aunt Laura would leave again. Fuck no, instead, it backfired and she got a job as a teacher in the high school.

But the voice — the Book — was speaking again.

~...*sssooooonnnn...yyyyooooouuuu wiiiillll haaaavvvve toooo reeeelinnnnquishhhh yyyyoooouuuurrrr hhhoooolllld onnnn mmmmeeee...*~

To who? she thought.

The Book didn't answer immediately, and Talia figured It was being its normal, annoyingly cryptic self again.

Then It spoke.

~...*toooo hhhhiiiimmmm...*~

She saw one of the other school pariahs walking down the hall, head down, greasy hair hanging limply over his pimpled face.

Him?

~...*yyyyeeeessss...*~

She found that hard to believe. But all hope left her just the same. She'd have to give up the Book to Stinky Pete Wilson? Really?

~...*YYYYEEEESSSS...*~

But why?

The Book did not respond with words this time. Instead, it showed her a terrifying creature of shadows. The Book made it clear It would not speak its name, but Talia got an impression...a gossamer wisp of knowledge.

The Dark Haunter of a Thousand Names and a Thousand Forms.

So it's not just You pulling the strings, she thought. *There's someone...some thing above you?*

~...*YYYYEEEESSSS...*~

Talia caught the eagerness — *or is it hunger?* — in the Book's tone.

And all at once she knew. She could tell by the way the Book seemed to strain against her to get to him. He was going to open up paths to hell that she'd only dreamed of.

And for the first time in a long time, Talia felt fear.

AUTHOR'S NOTE

I'VE ALWAYS BEEN a fan of the "behind the scenes" glimpse into what inspired the story the author wrote, so I figured, what the hell? Let's start a tradition.

So, where did *Bad Blood* come from?

It's a bit of a long story...

I had written *Out for Blood*—which is the full-length novel that comes immediately after this story, and that I hint at in the epilogue.

I had written the novel, and unsuccessfully shopped it around a bit, when I was approached by a small, Toronto-based press. The editor was looking to move beyond chapbooks (smaller works, essentially about 15 to 20-odd 8½ x 11 pages with teeny-tiny type, double-sided, folded in half, and stapled together) into novel-length works. And, she'd read *Out for Blood*—which I was calling *No Hope* at the time—and liked it enough to extend an offer to me.

To say I was excited would be an understatement. In fact, my daughter and I had been sitting at a table with the editor at Toronto's FanExpo, eating overpriced pizza as we talked. When the editor finally shook my hand and walked away, my daughter turned to me and said, "Wait, did I hear that right? Your novel's gonna get published?" We both sat in stunned silence for a few moments before breaking out in stupid grins. We toasted my success with horrifyingly expensive cups of Coca-Cola.

I should point out here that there's not a much greater feeling than celebrating a long-sought-after win with your equally-as-excited seventeen-year-old daughter.

So, I began the task of editing the hell out of the novel to get it ready for publication. This was right around 2008.

And then the automotive industry and banks went into the crapper.

The editor approached me, apologizing profusely, but explained, for a small press, this was rough. *Out for Blood* wouldn't be published that year as planned. Maybe the year after?

I completely understood, and continued to edit as I waited.

The next year wasn't much better. The novel still couldn't be published. But, the editor asked, what did I think of writing a novella-length work, perhaps something in the same world, or even a prequel to *Out for Blood*? Something to whet the appetite?

To tell the truth, I wasn't excited about that, because, quite frankly, I had nothing. But hey, it was still an offer to be published, so I wasn't about to turn it down.

I thought about some story ideas and dismissed them one by one.

Then, looking back at some of my written-but-as-yet-unpublished short stories for inspiration, I came across one called *The Wrong Child*, about a little girl named Cassie who had gone missing to play with a squirrel. She had a baby sister named Alex, who she was a little irked with, and an overworked mom. There was still a husband in the picture, but he didn't actually show up in the four-page, thousand-word story.

And I thought, *Yes, there's something here…*

The biggest change I made was to set the story in the town of New Hope. And to change Cassie's name to Talia. Why Talia, you ask?

Because Talia sits right in the middle of the word *retaliation*. As soon as it came to me, it was the only name for that little girl.

It actually didn't take long to flesh out the story, but I just didn't seem to have an ending for it.

I wrote about two-thirds of it, then got locked up. I didn't know how to finish it off.

It languished, unloved and ignored, in the bowels of my computer's memory.

The editor gently reminded me that there was a deadline coming up.

It took a while, but then I decided I had to come up with *some* way to finish it off. So, I started looking at each character in turn, and playing the "What if...?" game. That's when it came to me to make the dad...well, you know.

As soon as I had that plot point, the entire thing fell together easy as you please.

I wrote it up, we edited it, and we published it in time for the 2011 FanExpo, almost three years to the day from originally getting the offer.

The book was well-received, and it sold much better than I ever anticipated. And I was getting good reactions.

The editor held a reading at a bar in Toronto, and I chose the section toward the end, where Talia takes her vengeance out on Benji, the Kovacs's dog.

When I was up on stage, I was just focused on the reading. I wasn't really aware of what was going on beyond the page. But afterward a friend came up, a delighted smirk curling her lip, and told me that, when I got to the part about Benji's teeth, two women got up and abruptly ran from the room.

I couldn't have been more delighted.

Anyway, to wrap up this story, *Out for Blood* continued to be delayed a couple more years, and, unfortunately, once the editor was ready, I found there were some creative differences in our vision of what we wanted for the novel.

In the end, the editor was very professional and gracious and turned all the rights back to me for *Bad Blood* (which you may have read as *Vanishing Hope* if you're lucky enough to have snagged a copy).

Since then, my little novella prequel and novel ended up turning into more of a longer story arc. Which means those other stories had to be written, and then I had to come back and stitch in some connecting material here and there.

And now, we're starting the new journey. And here I would like to give a huge thank you to Jennifer Dinsmore, editor extraordinaire, for her keen eye and help in re-introducing Talia, and the Book — not to mention the entire Aphotic World — to the world.

Overall, this version of *Bad Blood* isn't a whole lot different from that one published back in 2011, but now, instead of whetting the appetite for a single-novel follow-up, it's toeing open the door on a much larger world.

You have the very first story in the world of The Book. I call these stories the *Aphotic World Cycle*.

The next one in the cycle, and the first full novel, *Out for Blood*, will come soon, followed by three more novels and one more novella — including a return of Talia at some point.

I have to say, I've had a hell of a lot of fun writing about this weird little town of New Hope and its people and environs, so I hope, as you come to visit, that you enjoy exploring this world as much as I did creating it.

ABOUT THE AUTHOR

TOBIN ELLIOTT HAS written for most of his life. After some unfortunate incidents with walls and permanent markers, he switched to safer things like pens and paper, and later, typewriters and then computers. Though science fiction was his first love, horror has always had a powerful hold on him, even back before he wore big-boy pants. He likes to have the shit scared out of him, and he likes scaring the shit out of others. Somehow, it always comes down to shit with Tobin.

Tobin spent his formative teenage years in a small town about four hours northeast of Toronto. Those experiences, and the magic and wonder of that place, never left him, though he left the town, through no fault of his own. He currently lives within a three-hour drive of the place, and occasionally gets back to top up on his sense of wonder and nostalgia.

Based on that town and surrounding areas, Tobin has written several novels in his Aphotic World series.

Along with those writings, Tobin has been fortunate enough to have had three horror novellas published, as well as seven stories in various anthologies. He has been a board member of both the Writers' Community of Simcoe County (WCSC) and the Writers' Community of Durham Region (WCDR), and, for five years, was an annual participant in the Muskoka Novel Marathon, a 72-hour writing marathon to raise money for adult literacy programs.

Finally, he also taught creative writing for two different continuous learning programs. Tobin writes ugly stories about bad people doing horrible things, and it was his pleasure to show other people how to do the same thing for almost twenty years.

If you're interested in more ramblings by Tobin, well, he's not much into social media. He sees it as a blight on humanity of almost Bookian proportions. And yet, still, he's on there.

Facebook: The Horror Guy (/TheHorrorGuy91)

Twitter: @TheHorrorGuy91

Instagram: @TheHorrorGuy91

◆ ◆ ◆

I HOPE THAT this book captured your imagination, and I hope that this series will turn you into a loyal reader.

Because loyal readers are an author's secret weapon. They can influence other readers...how?

Through reviews.

If you loved this book, and yes, even if you hated it, please also consider leaving a review on the site where you purchased it, and/or Goodreads, or anywhere else. You can also drop me a line at TheHorrorGuy91@gmail.com.

As a reader, you have an immense power to influence others.

Please, use that power.

CPSIA information can be obtained
at www.ICGtesting.com
Printed in the USA
LVHW101751271122
734106LV00002B/407